"I suppose you have a glamorous career?"

Jay's question caught her by surprise and Mirry found herself longing to impress him.

"Well, no," she had to admit. "For the last two years I've lived at home."

Before she could explain the reason, he said with a distinct sneer, "With five brothers to pander to your whims, you feel justified in living off your parents while you wait for your slice of the Wenlow estate?"

Mirry restrained her shocked indignation to say, "You believe attack is the finest form of defence, don't you? Just what is it you're defending yourself against, Jay?"

He didn't like her response but recovered quickly and said, "Oh, come now, you must all be hating my guts, the bastard you're having to share the loot with. So why are you all pretending the friendly welcome?"

STEPHANIE WYATT began writing soon after the birth of her daughter, in the intervals snatched between straining fruit and changing diapers, and in the past twenty years has had a number of short stories and several novels published. She and her husband live at the edge of a small village overlooking the rolling Leicestershire countryside, their one daughter having flown the nest.

Books by Stephanie Wyatt

HARLEQUIN PRESENTS
1054—THIS MAN'S MAGIC

STEPHANIE WYATT

friday's child

Harlequin Books

TORONTO • NEW YORK • LONDON
AMSTERDAM • PARIS • SYDNEY • HAMBURG
STOCKHOLM • ATHENS • TOKYO • MILAN

Harlequin Presents first edition March 1990
ISBN 0-373-11254-8

Original hardcover edition published in 1989
by Mills & Boon Limited

CHAPTER ONE

MARTHA BARKS didn't like people letting cold air into her warm kitchen, but the sight of the slender girl, her long, reddish hair rioting into curls from the frost, changed her frown to a smile of welcome. Mirry Grey had that effect on everyone. Compared to her handsome brothers she wasn't strictly pretty, but her small face had an animation that was more arresting than mere prettiness, the dancing brown eyes reflecting a zest for life that was infectious.

'Hi, Martha!' The girl stripped off her anorak. 'I've just had a call from Aunt Georgie. Very cryptic!'

The corners of Martha's mouth turned down. She had been housekeeper at Wenlow Hall since Lady Georgina Jayston had come there as a bride thirty-five years ago. Widowed twice during that time, she had very definite ideas of how the newly bereaved should behave, and her mistress was not conforming to those ideas.

'Got some bee in her bonnet. Helen says she had a restless night and she's been up since crack of dawn, racing all over the house.' Her mouth tightened further. 'Not the sort of thing you expect, with Sir David barely cold in his grave. Anyone'd think——'

'Everyone copes with grief their own way, Martha,' Mirry said quietly. 'And Aunt Georgie's never been one to weep and wail.'

After an inward battle Martha was forced to concede, 'No, that's never been her way.' She watched as Mirry

5

tugged off her boots. Such a tiny thing, little more than five feet tall while her brothers were all six feet and more. Though, of course, she was forgetting there was no actual blood relationship.

Mirry's wide mouth curved into a grin. 'Whatever she's planning has to be a good thing if it's giving her a new interest. Not making a show of it doesn't mean she's grieving any less.'

'Aye, love, I know,' Martha agreed. 'The kind of feeling they shared...' Her tone changed as she looked at Mirry accusingly. 'You, now—when are you going to stop taking on other people's problems and settle down with a man of your own?'

'I think the kind of man I'm looking for has gone out of fashion,' Mirry retorted, and she was only half joking. 'Now, I'd better try and find her. Any idea where she'll be?'

Martha's mouth turned down again. 'Well, she won't be in the attics. The lift doesn't go that far.'

Mirry laughed, pushing open the baize door that led to the front of the house, as familiar with the miles of corridors and endless rooms as she was with her own home. Bounding up the curving marble staircase, she was relieved to see Helen grinning at her from the door of the sitting-room that was part of the master suite. 'From what Martha said, I was expecting to chase you round for hours before I caught you.'

Helen gave a bark of laughter. 'And you would have, too, if I hadn't threatened to disconnect her motor.'

'Mirry, darling... I'm a monster, dragging you out on such a cold morning!' The rich contralto voice had Mirry crossing quickly to the electric wheelchair drawn up beside the fire. Years of pain had scored deep lines across

Georgina Jayston's face, but her blue eyes were bright with indomitable life.

'Nonsense! I'd be taking Nick to his speech therapy if Mum hadn't wanted to go into Leicester herself.' Mirry bent to kiss the powdered cheek beneath the halo of short white curls. 'How are you, Aunt Georgie?'

An honorary aunt only, Lady Georgina Jayston was actually Mirry's father's cousin, as well as her own dear godmother.

'All the better for seeing you, darling. Now poor Helen can have a break. I'm afraid I gave her a rough night. I was worrying, you see, then I had this marvellous idea...'

Mirry exchanged an understanding smile with Helen Dutton who, not much younger than her patient, had been Lady Georgie's nurse for at least ten years. Normally she lived in one of the cottages in the village, but since Sir David's death she had moved into the house.

'Yes, why don't you take the rest of the day off, Helen?' Mirry suggested. 'I can stay with Georgie.'

'Oh, but I couldn't expect——' Helen's protest was stifled by a yawn.

'You were saying?' Mirry's brown eyes danced. 'Helen, dear, if you don't go and put your feet up, I'll carry you out myself.'

A big, rawboned woman, Helen laughed at the ludicrous threat. 'You and whose army?' she challenged, then threw up her arms in surrender. 'All right, you bully, but you'll call me if you need me.'

'So what's this fantastic idea of yours?' Mirry asked as the door closed behind the nurse, sitting down and drawing the embroidery frame either she or Georgie were constantly working on towards her.

'Converting the wings of the house into flats,' Georgie returned promptly, and sat back to enjoy her god-daughter's reaction.

Accustomed as she was to Georgie's unconventional ideas, Mirry gaped. 'Aren't you being a mite ambitious? It would mean an awful lot of upset.'

'I don't intend to do the work myself, neither do I expect to live to see it finished.' Mirry made an involuntary sound of protest and, seeing her distress, Georgie added quickly, 'Oh, darling, don't look so unhappy. I've kept going for David's sake, but now he's gone...'

Tears brimmed in Mirry's eyes and, taking her hand, Georgie shook it in remonstration. 'No, you silly girl, I absolutely forbid you to cry. Look at it from my point of view, darling. To be free of pain, free of this wheelchair. To be with David for all eternity... Is that very selfish?'

Mirry dashed the tears from her eyes. 'Of course it isn't, and I do like to think of you and David being together again.' With a tremendous effort she attempted to lighten the atmosphere. 'Will you take to the harp or do you think they'll allow you your clarinet in heaven?'

Learning to play the clarinet had been one of Georgie's interests after imprisonment in a wheelchair had prematurely curtailed the active life she had loved, and over the years she had become a competent exponent, particularly of jazz, delighting in her god-daughter's shared interest and facility.

Mirry's remark struck just the right note and Georgie gurgled her amusement. 'Oh, Mirry, I wouldn't have missed having you in my life for anything! I love your brothers too, but you are something special. It just goes to show that environment is as important to a child as heredity.' She sobered quickly. 'Poor Jay wasn't so lucky.'

At this reference to Uncle David's son, Mirry looked startled, but said nothing as Georgie went on, 'He's not going to find it easy, stepping into his father's shoes without any preparation.'

Mirry and her family had always known that one day Wenlow would go to Jay Elphick, though none of them had expected it to happen for years yet. Sir David's sudden death two weeks ago at only sixty-four had stunned them all. 'I don't think you need to worry about that,' she said reassuringly.

'But I must.' Georgie's hands plucked at the armrests of her chair. 'I've always felt so guilty...'

Mirry stared. '*You've* felt guilty? Darling, you must be the one person who had *nothing* to reproach yourself for.'

'But I've always stood between David and his son,' she explained sadly. 'And between Jay and his rightful place here at Wenlow. But you must know the story.'

Mirry nodded. 'I know Valerie Elphick worked here for a while as Uncle David's secretary, that he— they——'

'I never blamed David,' Georgie said quickly. 'We'd been so much in love, shared such...*passion*. What are you blushing for, child? Your generation didn't invent sex, you know.'

Above her pink cheeks Mirry's brown eyes held an answering gleam. 'I *have* noticed Dad often can't keep his hands off Mum.'

'Yes, Donald's been very fortunate with his life-partner, too.' Georgie sighed. 'It was hard enough for me, remembering what we'd shared before I was paralysed, but it must have been impossible for a virile man like David to be tied to a woman who could no longer respond to him, let alone give him the children he wanted. Poor David.' Georgie's gaze was directed at the fire burning in the grate, but she was seeing the past. 'He was so wretched, so—so *shamed*. Valerie was demanding marriage to make the child legitimate. It seemed the best solution, so I offered to divorce him.'

'That was very brave of you,' Mirry said quietly, her tender heart wrung.

'He cried, Mirry.' There were tears in Georgie's eyes as she remembered. 'He told me it wasn't even infatuation, that Valerie was a woman of the world who'd offered him ease. He begged me on his knees not to leave him.'

'He loved you,' Mirry insisted.

'Yes, but he paid such a price, poor darling. He wanted the child so much. We both did. We pleaded with Valerie to let us adopt him, but she would never agree.'

Mirry knew that was when Uncle David had sold the Dower House to her father, settling the money on Valerie and her child.

'I don't think David ever quite gave up hope that Valerie might change her mind,' Georgie mused. 'Not for years and years.'

'But Uncle David used to see Jay sometimes,' Mirry prompted. 'I remember when I was small he used to talk to me about him. And then he suddenly stopped, and I never liked to ask...'

'That would be when Jay was eighteen and refused to have anything more to do with his father,' Georgie revealed. 'All we knew was that after university he got a job with a bank. I've no idea what position he holds now, but I doubt he has the means to put Wenlow back on its feet.'

At Mirry's startled glance she shrugged helplessly. 'Oh, I knew Valerie's demands over the years had been a drain on the estate—Odden Wood went, then Dicken's Farm—but I didn't know quite how bad things were until Mr Golding...' There were signs of strain on the lined face that Mirry guessed were put there by the visits the solicitor had made since David's death.

She marvelled that Georgie could be so concerned for a man whose very existence had cause her so much pain. 'So this is where your idea comes in, then?' she prompted.

Georgie sat up straighter. 'Well, it occurred to me that if the house itself could provide an income... All those empty rooms. Mirry, I want you to do a survey and draw up some plans for me.'

'Me?' She was taken aback. 'But you know it takes seven years to become an architect, and I only did two.'

'You advised Jessica and Rory about enlarging the tea-rooms, and your plans were passed by the council.'

'Well, yes,' Mirry conceded. 'But that was very straightforward...'

'I don't see that this will be that much more compli-cated,' Georgie persisted. 'It would involve building walls rather than knocking them down. I've been looking round this morning and I'm sure it could be done.'

'Well, of course it could, but do you really think I'm the right person to——'

'I never thought to see the day when Mirry Grey was afraid to face a challenge.'

And, just as her godmother expected, Mirry looked affronted. 'Of course I'm not afraid, I just——'

'Good, in that case you'll have no objections to coming with me now to take a look.' Expertly, Georgie swung the wheelchair towards the door.

Two hours later, lunching on one of Martha's delicious pies, Georgie asked innocently, 'Well, Mirry, what do you think?'

Seeing right through that spurious innocence, Mirry grinned. 'I think you're a wily old witch. You know very well I'm hooked on the idea.'

Her godmother's smile was complacent. 'This wily old witch has been even more forward-thinking. Have you realised this could be the beginning of a new career for you? Well, you've been telling me how doubtful you are of picking up your studies again after so long.'

Mirry chewed thoughtfully. It was an idea. Now Nick was so much improved, she would soon have to consider her future. 'You do realise a conversion of this size can't be done for peanuts, Aunt Georgie? If the estate's in such a bad way, will you be able to raise the money?'

Georgie relaxed now she had Mirry's agreement. 'I have some money of my own that David always refused to touch. Wenlow is Jay's heritage. I can't change the past, but I can try to ensure his future.' She reached across the table to clasp Mirry's hand. 'Mirry, you've always known how much you were wanted and valued, known the love of parents and family, when it might have been very different. You of all people should be able to feel for him.'

Mirry could. However much Jay's mother had loved him, it couldn't make up for the lack of a father, for close family ties, that sense of belonging. She nodded. 'There, but for the grace of God...'

Her answer seemed to lift a weight from her god-mother's shoulders. 'I knew you'd understand. What's that line in that old nursery rhyme? "Friday's child is loving and giving..." I don't know anyone it applies to more aptly, Mirry. I know you'll make Jay feel welcome, convince him Wenlow is his rightful place, that he was always wanted here.'

Mirry felt the tears pricking behind her eyes because Georgie was talking of the time when she would no longer be here. But she blinked them back, telling herself it wouldn't be for years yet.

It was barely nine weeks later, and on the day of the funeral Mirry woke to find the weather too was mourning, the March wind rattling the rain against the windows to run down the glass like the tears she had promised not to shed.

She had overslept too, which wasn't surprising considering the time she had got to bed. Flinging back the duvet, she crawled out of bed and walked blearily through the connecting door, dragging off her pink satin nightshirt.

Built in the time of the early Tudors, the Dower House had in fact been the original Hall. It had been a Jacobean Jayston who, tiring of a house where room led haphazardly out of room, had built the present Wenlow Hall. When all her brothers had still been at home and their family swelled still further by the many foster brothers and sisters who had shared their childhood, this smaller room that led out of Mirry's had been a bedroom, but several years ago it had been converted into her own bathroom.

A few minutes under the shower made Mirry feel more human, and, hurrying into jeans and sweater, she went downstairs, pattering along the stone-floored passage to what had once been the dairy and was now a small gym.

The harsh strip-lighting illuminated the face of the young man on the exercise machine, his face set in a rictus of concentration as he tried to co-ordinate his movements. Her appearance distracted him and the weight that balanced the tension bar fell with a crash. 'Sorry, Nick, but it's time you finished anyway.' He no longer needed her to supervise his exercise sessions, but she liked to make sure he didn't overdo things.

But Nick's jaw jutted pugnaciously and a steam of unintelligible protest burst from him, the words jumbling together as they still did when he was under pressure. Mirry laid a calming hand on his shoulder. Nick was the youngest of her five brothers, and the one nearest to her in age, at twenty-four little more than a year her senior. They had always been close, but since his accident they hardly needed words. She knew what he was trying to say, but reading his thoughts wasn't part of the therapy. 'Whoa there, Tiger! Take it slowly, huh?'

Nick took a deep breath. 'Want to try again, Mirry, get it right.' The words were still slurred, but this time intelligible.

Pride and affection sparkled in Mirry's eyes. And this was the same Nick who, two years ago, the doctors had declared would never be more than a cabbage! 'OK, just once, then breakfast.'

Nick took a fresh grip, slid his feet into the stirrups and began again, and this time, for twelve counts, the thumps were evenly spaced.

'I did it, Mirry!' A triumphant grin lit his handsome face, and for a few moments it could have been the Nick of two years ago, with the future his good looks and high intelligence had promised. Only when he extricated himself clumsily from the exercise machine and lurched as he moved to hug her was the illusion dashed.

'Didn't I always say you could?' A slight huskiness betrayed the emotions constricting her throat as she hugged him back, her cheek pressing against his damp T-shirt. 'Ugh!' She pretended disgust at his sweat-soaked body. 'You'd better get your shower.'

She sighed as she watched his shambling gait as he left the room. Her constant companion during their growing up years, it had been Nick who had spurred her own ambitions to opt for a career still weighted against females. He'd even wanted to defer his scholarship to Cambridge for a year until Mirry would be ready to leave for university. Perhaps if she hadn't talked him out of that idea he wouldn't have been in the wrong place at the wrong time...

But it was no good thinking of might-have-beens. Nick's accident had happened, cutting short both their careers, because there had been no question of Mirry pursuing her dream of becoming an architect when Nick needed her.

After the dairy, the big, old-fashioned kitchen was cosy.

'Just look at the weather!' Mirry said in disgust, ruffling Andrew's already wind-tousled hair and dropping a kiss on her father's cheek as they both sat at the big table.

'Don't knock it,' Donald Grey grinned. 'Good growing weather; at least, it would be if it'd warm up a bit.'

'All right for your precious plants, but what about Aunt Georgie's sofa?' Mirry's smile belied her grumbling tone.

'You finished it, then?' her mother asked from the stove.

'Two o'clock this morning.' Mirry reached up to kiss her cheek. Cathy Grey was small compared to her husband and five hulking sons, but Mirry was smaller, the top of her head barely reaching her mother's ear. With her reddish-brown hair tumbling down her back she looked no more than sixteen, especially as the curves which were a clue to her actual twenty-three years were hidden by her bulky sweater.

'Oh, darling...' Cathy Grey's still pretty face clouded with compunction. 'Maybe I shouldn't have pushed you...'

'What was the rush, anyway?' Andrew reached for the coffee-pot to refill his cup.

Mirry noticed her mother's troubled frown. 'I'll have some coffee, please, Andrew. And Mum's right. The sooner the sofa's returned to the house, the better.'

'I still don't see it matters.' Andrew filled her cup. 'Jay Elphick's had one of his heirlooms restored, after all.'

Cathy and Donald exchanged a look of understanding as she took his empty plate and received a caressing pat on her still neat posterior. Though her dark hair was sprinkled with grey and his was fast disappearing, their love was expressed in many such ways every day of their lives.

'You'll need the truck, then, Mirry,' her father said. 'Do you want Andrew too, to help with the lifting?'

'I can do it.' Nick, his hair still damp, had caught the last part of the conversation. 'I often help Mirry.'

'That's right, Nick. You're the brains and I'm the brawn.' Mirry grinned, then, turning to her father, added, 'Of course Nick and I can manage. It's only a little sofa and anyway I'm——'

'—stronger than you look,' Donald and Andrew chorused, picking up the old family joke.

After helping her mother with the chores, Mirry went out to the back lobby, grabbing the first anorak that came to hand. It hung well below her knees, the hood falling over her nose, which wasn't a bad thing as the rain-filled wind buffeted her.

There were already a few cars in the garden centre car park, and the small craft showrooms converted from former outhouses were open for business. They were well established; the unit Mirry unlocked contained only her drawing-board and tools, but it was where she had begun to dream of establishing her own business.

Although doubtful of her capabilities at first, the longer she had worked on the conversion project the more enthusiastic she had become. Georgie had been delighted with her plans, and Mirry had needed little encouragement to complete the specifications. But there had been no time to submit the finished plans to the local council. Aunt Georgie had gone to bed one night a week ago and had failed to wake up in the morning.

So Mirry's new career was already in limbo. There would be nothing to stop Jay Elphick going along with the plans when he took over at Wenlow, but she doubted he'd consider a partly trained architect with no experience capable of handling the job. Sighing, she stripped off her anorak.

If Jay was coming into his inheritance too soon to find the upkeep of the house supported by the rents from the luxury flats as Georgie had planned, at least he would find the extensive collection of Jacobean needlework almost completely restored. It had begun ten years ago when Mirry had copied the pattern on one of the bed-hangings to make a picture. That first attempt had been very amateur, but it had caught Aunt Georgie's interest. Mirry had copied more of the patterns, and after months of practising the different stitches they had embarked on the task of restoring the original needlework.

The little sofa had been one of the last pieces, not only the pattern worn away but the fabric itself in shreds. Mirry had started from scratch, selecting from the many authentic designs of birds and beasts and flowers she had collected over the years. She had completed the embroidery but not the re-upholstery when Georgie had died, and it had been her mother's insistence that it should be finished and returned to the Hall before Jay's arrival that had been the cause of Mirry's late night.

She found herself speculating curiously about this unknown cousin as she wrapped the sofa in air-bubble plastic to protect it, feeling a tingle of excitement that she would soon meet him.

Andrew backed the truck up to the door and helped Nick stow the sofa aboard. Pulling on the over-large anorak again, Mirry clambered into the cab beside Nick and drove out on to the narrow road that wound between high hedges just beginning to show a tender green. In less than five hundred yards she was slowing again, turning by the tiny church into a drive that curved beside a shallow lake up to a large, honey-stuccoed house.

The rain spattered against the plastic covering as they carried the sofa into the house, the hood of Mirry's anorak covering so much of her face she could only see her feet. But she knew every inch of the house and unerringly led the way across the great hall into the inner hall and started up the curving staircase.

After three steps there was a jerk as Nick stumbled. 'Sorry,' he muttered, butting her in the back as he moved forward again, bearing her along too fast to negotiate the bend. Nick grunted as the sofa became wedged between the wall and the iron balustrade.

Clawing the impeding hood back far enough to survey the problem, she directed breathlessly, 'Back up, Nick. No...gently!'

'What the devil do you think you're doing?' a harsh voice grated, and they both jumped, Nick turning to gaze mutely at the speaker, Mirry peering over the balustrade to get an impression of light brown hair trimmed neatly against a well-shaped head, and a lean body clad in a formal grey business suit.

'Wherever you were going with that, you'll take it back...at once.' He spoke quietly, but with a ring of authority that had Nick glancing at Mirry for guidance. Snapping out of her trance, she said, 'I'm sorry, but we didn't expect——'

He ignored her, firing at Nick, 'What are you, gypsies come to see what the pickings are?'

Mirry gasped, but, frustrated by the sofa blocking her way, she had to listen as he said threateningly to Nick, 'Are you going to put it back, or do I have to make you?'

'Now, look, if you'd only let me explain——' Mirry tried again. This time he did deign to look at her, and she felt a sharp jolt. The eyes that were regarding her so scathingly were a light silvery grey, the coldest eyes she had ever seen.

Used all her life to affectionate indulgence from the male sex, she was even more shattered when he said rudely, 'I was talking to the organ grinder, not the monkey,' and turned his inimical gaze back to Nick. 'I assume it *is* you and not your little brother who is in charge of this operation?' And when Nick still said nothing, 'Well? Are you dumb as well as daft?'

Nick's hands curled into fists as he struggled to answer, finally bursting into an unintelligible stream of words.

'My God, it's the bloody village idiot!'

Fury at the callous remark gave Mirry the impetus to shove at the sofa until she could squeeze past. 'Nick...' She stood protectively between her brother and his attacker. 'Wait for me in the truck.'

Nick cast an apprehensive glance at the man who snapped, 'Oh, no, you don't. You're neither of you——'

'Shut up!' Mirry turned on him like a bantam cock, sweeping the hampering hood from her head so the reddish curls tumbled wildly about her face. His surprise would have been laughable had she not been so angry. 'Tell me, Mr Elphick, do you jeer at cripples, too?'

The silvery eyes narrowed. 'You know my name?'

Mirry refused to be side-tracked. 'If my brother had lost an arm or a leg, would you still be calling him names?' Not allowing the discomfited man to answer, she powered on, her temper lost beyond recall, 'To set the matter straight, we were *not* trying to make off with one of your heirlooms. We were in fact returning it after restoration. It belongs in the sitting-room of the master suite, and how you're going to get it there now is your problem.'

Taking advantage of the fact that her diatribe had momentarily stunned her antagonist, she dragged Nick past him in a flurry of billowing anorak and flying hair.

CHAPTER TWO

CLIMBING into the truck, Mirry wondered how she was going to reassure her brother, but to her surprise his expression showed only admiring wonder.

'You sure told him, Mirry.' His speech was relatively clear now and his mouth twitched in amusement.

'I wasn't having him call you an idiot,' she muttered, 'which is why I——'

'—went for the jugular,' Nick finished with a grin. 'Poor chap didn't know what hit him.'

Mirry looked at him in consternation. So much for the understanding welcome Georgie had trusted her to give to Jay! 'I did go over the top a bit, didn't I? Should I go back?'

Nick shook his head, grinning. 'He'd probably hide.'

Mirry worried about it as she drove the short distance home, but as she parked beside a sedate grey BMW, a throaty roar from a racy red sports car sweeping up behind them put everything else out of her mind.

'Simon!' Nick scrambled out of the truck and Mirry followed suit, hurtling to greet the most handsome of her five good-looking brothers.

'Hi, Nick . . . Mirry . . .' Simon peered at the all-enveloping anorak. 'I assume it *is* my little sister in there somewhere.' He swept her off her feet in a hug and Mirry squealed with pleasure.

Asking excited questions, she led the way into the house and through to the sitting-room where the fitful sunlight and leaded window-panes were making crossword patterns on the polished floor. There they found Richard and his blonde wife Sandra drinking coffee with their mother.

After the delighted greetings, Cathy said, 'You've been quick, Mirry.'

Nick enunciated carefully, 'We had a run-in with Jay Elphick and thought we'd better come back and tell you.'

'He's here *today*!' Cathy said incredulously.

'Jay Elphick?' Sandra sat up, her blonde hair swinging. 'What's he like, Mirry? Too awful? To think of some little bank clerk taking Sir David's place!'

Richard avoided his mother's gaze as he remonstrated mildly, 'Don't be such a snob, Sandra.'

Mirry was aware they were waiting for her opinion, but what could she say? Cold as marble with a burn like dry ice? Certainly nothing like the humble bank clerk of Sandra's imagining. 'I think you could be in for a surprise,' she told her sister-in-law.

'I'm surprised he's turned up for the funeral, since he didn't attend his father's,' Cathy said tartly. 'Was he alone?'

'I didn't see anyone else.' And hadn't waited to find out!

'I wondered if his mother was with him.' Cathy grimaced. 'Now, I *could* imagine her eager to be at Georgie's funeral—to dance!'

Her unfamiliar bitterness had all five young people staring. 'Which would have been better unsaid,' she conceded. 'I'd better phone Martha to see if everything can still go ahead as arranged.'

That was a complication that hadn't occurred to Mirry, and her relief was as great as her mother's when Cathy returned to say, 'It's all right, Jay arrived today on the solicitor's instructions. Unfortunately Mr Golding omitted to tell him about the funeral. But Martha says he doesn't want to interfere. She also says...' she fixed a puzzled gaze on her daughter '...to tell Mirry Mr Elphick managed to get the sofa upstairs all right. Mirry, what's been going on?'

Her face flamed and she shot an agonised glance at the grinning Nick. 'He appeared like a genie just as we got the sofa stuck on the stairs, and jumped to the conclusion we were stealing it,' she told them uncomfortably. 'He wouldn't listen when I tried to explain. In fact, he was pretty nasty to Nick.'

'So she told him what she thought of him and stormed out,' Nick added with huge enjoyment.

Richard and Simon roared with laughter, for both had baited their sister in the past and knew what a firebrand she could be. But Mirry was recalling her mother's bitterness towards Jay's mother. It wasn't until she was in the kitchen, slicing breadsticks and spreading the garlic butter, that she was able to ask, 'You don't resent Jay's inheriting Wenlow, do you, Mum?'

Her mother's hand slowed as she stirred the pan. 'He is David's only son, and Georgie always wanted it, too.'

Mirry tore off strips of tinfoil, sensing her mother's reservations. She already regretted over-reacting to Jay's remarks, now she was beginning to regret telling her family about it if it was going to cause more ill-feeling. 'I know I got off on the wrong foot with Jay, but I can't help feeling sorry for him. He's missed out on such a lot, hasn't he?' She was thinking how different her own life might have been if she hadn't been lucky enough to become part of her big, affectionate family.

She surprised a shamed expression on her mother's face. 'I should think he's missed out on everything that matters,' Cathy agreed. 'I was forgetting Jay was a victim of his mother's ambitions, too.' She hesitated. 'You knew David and Georgie wanted to adopt him?'

Mirry nodded. 'But you can't blame Valerie for wanting to keep him.'

'Oh, Mirry...' Cathy shook her head. 'Valerie Elphick was no naïve girl losing her head over a married man. She was already in her late twenties, a failed marriage behind her and as hard as nails. David was the vulnerable one and she played on that. Her pregnancy was deliberate. She thought if she produced the son his wife couldn't give him, David would marry her.'

It was the first time Mirry had ever heard her mother speak ill of anyone, which made it all the more convincing, but she still felt bound to protest, 'You can't be sure of that, Mum.'

'Can't I? When she told David the only way he was going to see his child was if he married her?' Cathy slammed the tray of breadsticks into the oven. 'Mirry, you have no idea what it was like, the threats... She was going to abort the baby, to have it adopted by strangers, go abroad and just abandon it. Anything to get David to change his offer of adoption to one of marriage. Poor David was going out of his mind, but I knew if she got rid of the child she'd no longer have a bargaining point. And in the end she settled for the money when David sold the Dower House to us. His only stipulation was that she allowed him access, and she did let him visit her as often as he liked at first, obviously hoping the child would help to change his mind. But when that didn't work she began to make difficulties, rationing his visits and——'

'—using the baby as a weapon,' Mirry said with a shudder.

Her mother nodded. 'David and Georgie hoped she'd tire of the game eventually, and allow the adoption, but it went on and on, with Valerie getting more and more hostile, telling the boy his father didn't want him.'

Mirry was appalled that any mother could raise such confusion in a child's mind. 'But surely as Jay grew older David must have been able to tell him——'

Her mother's laugh was devoid of humour. 'Valerie never once let David see his son unless she was present. And David had too many scruples to drag the boy into the battle. Now can you understand why I can only view her triumphal return here with dread?'

'But she *isn't* here yet,' Mirry pointed out.

Her mother relaxed. 'No. At least it gives us the chance to get to know Jay without her disruptive influence.'

By two o'clock that afternoon Mirry was unrecognisable as the urchin who'd clashed with Jay Elphick. Severe brushing had brought out the red lights in her hair and had tamed it into a sleek chignon with only a few errant tendrils escaping. Her elegant black suit was a world away from the swamping anorak, the narrow skirt hugging her hips, the nipped-in waist emphasising the swell of her breasts, while the frothy ruffles of her chiffon blouse softened the tailored look. Black patent shoes on her narrow feet added three inches to her diminutive height, and a pert black pillbox hat completed the transformation.

Mirry was too busy trying to control the lump in her throat to care what a delicately elegant picture she made as the family and friends of Lady Georgina Jayston gathered at Wenlow to follow her on her last short journey. As if it had used up all its spite that morning, the weather had cleared and the sun shone on the cortège as it moved on foot down the drive to the tiny church at the gates.

Mirry fought hard to maintain her composure during the simple service, but lost it completely when her beloved godmother was finally laid to rest beside her husband in the family vault. By the time Simon and Nick had helped her to recover, they were the last to return to the Hall, where they found the family solicitor standing with a poker-faced Jay Elphick, introducing him to each mourner in turn.

'Ah, Simon and the two youngest members of the Grey family, Nicholas and Mirry,' Mr Golding said affably, and again there was that strangely shocking jolt as she looked up into those cold grey eyes.

As Simon said, 'I understand you met my sister this morning,' those eyes raked her from head to toe. 'Richard and I fell about laughing when we heard she'd left you with a sofa stuck half-way up the stairs,' Simon went on irrepressibly. 'But then, the temper goes with the red in her hair. I must say it's great to meet you at last, Jay.'

Some of the stiffness left Jay's expression, an element of uncertainty creeping in. That slight loosening up made Mirry realise he was actually very attractive—without her brothers' ruggedness but with good bone-structure, high cheekbones, a straight nose and slightly jutting eyebrows that shadowed those cold grey eyes. He held himself proudly, with a touch of aggressiveness in the tilt of his chin. Not a face to reveal emotion, though; guarded.

Her gaze had reached his mouth as he made some polite reply to Simon. It was the only feature he had inherited from his father. Like Sir David's it was full, well cut, though the way he tucked in the corners gave him a buttoned-up look. Unlike David's, it was a mouth that looked as if it didn't laugh much.

Simon moved away but Mr Golding detained Mirry. 'I thought it advisable to get the reading of the will over today. In the dining-room in an hour?' As Mirry nodded her agreement he went on, 'Well, Mr Elphick, Mirry knows everyone here so I'll leave you in her capable hands.'

He wandered off and Mirry took the opportunity to make her overdue apology. 'I'm sorry for flying at you this morning, Jay, but I'm sure you can understand how sensitive I am where Nick's concerned.'

Again the silvery gaze raked over her. 'No one could mistake you for a gypsy this afternoon, Miss Grey.' His gaze moved to Nick, who still stood behind her. 'If apologies are the order of the day, then I owe you mine, Nick. My remarks were uncalled for and your sister was justifiably upset. I can only say I'm sorry if you were hurt, and ask you to forgive me.'

A grin spread over Nick's face. 'Sure, Jay. Mirry'n' me, we talked about you coming to Wenlow... hoped we'd be friends.'

That Jay understood Nick's speech, slurred though it was, was apparent in the derisive eyebrows he raised at Mirry. 'Did you, indeed? And I was cloddish enough to give you the worst possible impression of my manners.'

Mirry was embarrassed by Nick's guileless confession, but relieved enough by the warming of the atmosphere to concede ruefully, 'We couldn't have made a good impression, either.' Feeling the need to explain her brother's problem, she added, 'Nick can cope with most things now, but still has trouble with his speech.'

'The words sort of jam up.' Nick's boyish face lit up. 'I say, Martha's bringing on the eats.'

As he made a beeline for the housekeeper, Jay asked abruptly, 'What happened to him? I gather from your remarks this morning he wasn't born handicapped.'

'No, Nick was probably the brightest of all my brothers. He was knocked off his bicycle by a drunken driver.' Again Mirry felt the wash of futile anger and took a deep breath. 'The doctors said he would always be a cabbage, but we proved them wrong.'

'*All* your brothers? How many do you have, then?'

'Five. I——'

'Five?' He stared at her disbelievingly.

'You sound as if you don't approve of large families,' Mirry challenged. 'I can assure you we were all wanted, and Mum and Dad had enough love to spare for numerous foster children, too.'

A strange look slid from behind the poker-faced mask Jay seemed to wear habitually. 'I didn't intend to criticise. It sounds great, to be part of a large family.' The note of wistfulness Mirry detected made him seem more approachable, and when he went on, 'I've been introduced to them, obviously, but with so many people... Would you point them out to me again?'

She found herself complying with all her natural warmth. 'That's William, by the fireplace. He's the eldest—thirty-seven. He's a consultant gynaecologist and obstetrician. Eleanor, the dark girl with him, was a physiotherapist before they married. It's thanks to her that Nick's made such a wonderful recovery.' Her affection for her favourite sister-in-law was unconsciously revealed in her voice.

She let her gaze move further round the room. 'The next one's Richard. That's him over there by the door.'

'The one with the gorgeous blonde?' Jay asked.

'The gorgeous blonde is his wife, Sandra,' Mirry said sharply.

He looked down at her from his poker-face. 'It can't be because I admired her that put the lemons in your voice. Don't you like the beauteous Sandra?'

'Of course I do.' Then honesty prompted her to confess, 'But not as much as Eleanor. Richard's an engineer, runs his own firm. Simon comes next. He's an airline pilot and lives in London.'

'And let me guess . . . unmarried?'

Mirry was surprised into bubbling laughter. 'Does it show? He's probably disappeared with the prettiest girl he can find. Now, that's Andrew.' She put a hand on his arm to draw him aside where he had a clear view of Andrew doggedly talking to the Frosts while their daughter Annabel was just as doggedly trying to ignore him.

'He's not married either, though he's trying to interest the girl he's with.' The Frosts ran the local riding stables, and during her teen years the lovestruck Annabel had dogged the embarrassed and evasive Andrew's footsteps. Only when he had brought a girl home with him from horticultural college had she relinquished her hopeless love, taking herself off to work as a stable girl on a stud farm on the other side of the country. She had left a coltish schoolgirl and returned a tall, lithe, confident young woman who seemed not to notice Andrew's stunned expression on seeing her again, or to set much store by his frequent excuses to call at the Frost place. Mirry suspected Annabel wasn't as indifferent to Andrew as she appeared, but who could blame her for punishing him a little?

Poor Andrew's dilemma put a sparkle into Mirry's brown eyes, something that seemed to fascinate her companion. 'Andrew is my father's partner in the garden centre. Nick helps there, too.' Some of her sparkle died. 'Nick was the brightest of them all,' she went on sadly. 'He was at Cambridge and was due to take his finals when that car put an end to everything.'

'So where do you come in the family?' Jay wanted to know.

'At the tail end.' Mirry grinned. 'I'm twenty-three, only a year younger than Nick, but he never lets me forget I'm the baby.'

'This morning I'd have called you a liar, but this afternoon...' his gaze lingered on the swell of her breasts '...I can believe it.'

It was as if he had touched her where his glance rested, quickening her heartbeat, tingling her skin, making her breasts ache for something nameless.

Growing up with five brothers, Mirry believed herself to be knowledgeable in the ways of men. In fact, for a modern girl she was unusually inexperienced. Of course, she had flirted with her brothers' friends, had laughingly enjoyed their kisses. But nothing had prepared her for the oddly disturbing sensations just a look from Jay Elphick aroused.

'I suppose you have an equally glamorous career,' he said, and Mirry found herself longing to impress him, but had to admit, 'Well, no. For the last two years I've lived at home.'

Before she could explain the reason, he said with a distinct sneer, 'With five brothers to pander to your whims, you feel justified in living off your parents while you wait for your slice of the Wenlow estate?'

Mirry's initial reaction was shocked indignation, but with a superhuman effort she managed to rein it in. 'You do believe attack is the finest form of defence, don't you?' she said reflectively. 'Just what is it you're defending yourself against, Jay?'

Her restraint paid off because she could see he hadn't been prepared for it, nor did he like it. But he recovered quickly, that beautiful mouth curving into the semblance of a smile, while the silvery eyes remained contemptuous. 'Oh, come now, The estimable Mrs Barks informed me the Greys at the Dower House were Lady Jayston's only relatives. *Legitimate* relatives. And you must all be hating my guts, the bastard you're having to share the loot with. So why are you all pretending the friendly welcome?'

Privately Mirry thought some people were bastards by an accident of birth, while others were bastards by nature, but aloud she said gently, 'Jay, we've always known about you, and that Wenlow would be yours one day, so as none of us ever had any expectations, why on earth would we hate you? I'm sorry you——'

But before she could go on a feminine voice complained, 'Mirry, you are a beast, keeping Jay to yourself when we're all dying to talk to him.'

Tall and athletic, Annabel Frost always made Mirry feel like a shrimp. Shaking back her glossy fair hair, she smiled flirtatiously at Jay, and Mirry watched as the poker-faced, buttoned-up expression melted, the fascinating mouth curving into a genuine smile that even reached those silvery-grey eyes as he responded to Annabel's approach.

The two girls had always had a friendly relationship, but at that moment she wished Annabel a thousand miles away. Instead she said politely, 'I'm sure you've already been introduced to Annabel, Jay.'

'Ah, yes, you run the riding stables, I believe.'

'You must have a phenomenal memory to remember that when you've met so many people today,' Annabel said admiringly. 'Actually, I was working on a stud farm near Newmarket until...'

Mirry moved away and neither of them noticed.

CHAPTER THREE

GOOD manners kept Mirry chatting and smiling, while inside she felt she had received a public slap. Of course she couldn't blame Jay for preferring the much prettier Annabel's company, but she was puzzled and hurt by his open antagonism.

She was jerked out of her abstraction when a deep voice redolent of the Canadian prairies said, 'I kept wondering who the mysterious pocket Venus in black was until I heard her laugh.'

'Keir!' Mirry's face lit up, unaware that her laughing surprise had Jay's head turning to look. 'I thought you were still in Canada. Where's Abigail?'

He moved his large frame sideways, hooking his arm about a roundly pregnant young woman making a smiling remark to the vicar. 'Never farther from me than I can help. Look who I've found, Abby. Young Mirry masquerading as a sophisticated woman of the world.'

'Take no notice of his teasing, Mirry, you look wonderful.' Abigail Minto's accent was uncompromisingly English.

Mirry flushed with pleasure at the compliment. 'I don't have to ask how you are, Abby, obviously blooming. I can't imagine how I missed seeing you earlier.' She laughed. 'There's certainly more of you than there was a month ago. How was Canada?'

'Wonderful!' The glance Abby exchanged with her husband suggested that, in spite of her being almost six

months pregnant, the trip had been something of a
second honeymoon. 'The flying was tiring but my in-
laws have been spoiling me rotten.' The smile in her dark
eyes faded to be replaced by intense regret. 'But we had
to come back as soon as we heard about Georgie. We
owe her so much, don't we, darling?'

'I'll say!' Keir agreed. 'She had such a zest for life, it
was only too easy to forget she was tied to that wheelchair.' He grinned. 'Who but Georgie could have weaned
my wife from her classical music and given her an interest
in jazz?'

'Which reminds me——' Abby broke in. 'What about
the send-off the jazz club is giving Georgie tonight? Have
you asked the new heir if it can still go ahead?'

Dismay was written clearly on Mirry's vivid face. 'Oh,
grief! I forgot all about it.'

'No sweat,' Keir said easily. 'We'll go and ask him
now. Is he staying overnight?'

'I've no idea.' For the first time since walking away
from him, Mirry allowed her glance to seek Jay out, a
hollow feeling in her stomach when she saw he was still
in close conversation with Annabel, who was sparkling
up at him as if she'd found the crock of gold at the end
of the rainbow.

'You were talking to him all that time and never asked
him his plans?' Abby asked curiously.

'He—he was asking about the family.' She grimaced.
'I don't think he likes us.'

'Oh, come on, honey,' Keir protested. 'How could he
know on such short acquaintance? And what's to dislike,
for pity's sake?'

'Thanks for the commendation, Keir.' Mirry managed
a wry grin. 'All the same, I think you're more likely to

get his permission to use the music-room tonight than I am.'

Keir's eyebrows nearly disappeared into the dark fall of hair across his brow, but it was Abby who expressed their curiosity. 'What on earth *did* go on between you, Mirry? I've never known you take an instant dislike to anyone before.'

'I don't dislike him,' Mirry denied at once. In fact, as she watched the genuine amusement on his face as Annabel flirted openly with him, she was startled to admit her overriding emotion was envy. 'Let's just say I'm wary of crossing swords with him again.'

'Curiouser and curiouser!' Abby murmured. 'Come on, Keir, I can't wait to meet the man who has such an effect on our Mirry.' Her brown eyes full of mischief she added to Mirry, 'I'll report my findings later.'

Pretending a complete lack of interest, Mirry was nevertheless aware that Annabel didn't welcome the Mintos' intrusion, nor could she help noticing the growing interest in Keir's face as the two men talked, or close her ears to the laughter of four people getting on well together. And she wasn't the only one who felt out of it, she realised, catching sight of Andrew as he too watched from across the room.

Was Annabel turning the screw on Andrew a little more, or was she genuinely attracted to Jay? Mirry wondered, then saw the solicitor join the group and Jay make his excuses. It was time to go to the dining-room for the reading of Georgie's will.

As Mirry crossed the room, Abby intercepted her. 'I don't know what you found so alarming about him, Mirry. He was a bit stiff at first, but he soon loosened up.' Her eyes widened in a look of innocence. 'Annabel certainly finds him charming.'

'Because he put himself out to charm her,' Mirry said wryly. 'He didn't trouble with me.'

'I wonder why not?' Abby's tone was speculative as she eyed her friend. 'Oh, Annabel's attractive enough, but you, Mirry—you look good enough to eat.'

'Thank you, but your partiality's showing.' Mirry laughed disbelievingly, then, as Helen Dutton hovered at her elbow, added, 'Shall I see you later?'

'Tonight,' Abby said. 'Jay has no objections to us using the music-room, in fact he was rather intrigued.'

Jay was already at the long table when Mirry and the nurse walked into the dining-room, Martha Barks sitting at a respectful distance. He didn't even turn his head to acknowledge her arrival. Mr Golding saw them seated then cleared his throat, rustled his papers and began, the legal phrases rolling off his tongue.

First there was the bequest to the long-serving house-keeper, which meant Martha could retire if she wished. Likewise Helen Dutton. Then Mr Golding continued, 'And to my beloved god-daughter, Georgina Catherine Grey...' Her head bowed, she was still aware that Jay twisted suddenly in his chair, his eyes burning into her.

Mr Golding went on to enumerate the pieces of jewellery Mirry knew so well. 'We'll check them off against the list when all the legalities have been completed, Mirry,' he suggested, and she nodded, aware again of Jay's sudden movement.

Afraid he might make another of his snide remarks, she stood up, breaking into Mr Golding's portentous, 'And now we come to the main bequest——'

'Forgive me, Mr Golding, but as the rest doesn't concern us, perhaps Martha, Helen and I should leave?'

Helen immediately got to her feet, Martha more slowly and much more reluctantly.

'Yes . . . yes, of course.' Courteously, the solicitor rose to escort the two older women to the door.

Mirry moved to follow when she heard Jay say in a stinging undertone, 'Cutting and running with the loot, Miss Grey?'

Mirry stopped dead, this fresh attack making her feel more hurt than angry. Facing him with unconscious dignity, she said quietly, 'The "loot" is some personal jewellery of Lady Jayston's. Besides being my godmother, she and my father were first cousins with a grandmother in common. It's *her* jewellery I've inherited—my great-grandmother's. I'm sure Mr Golding will be able to tell you the Jayston heirlooms have all been kept intact for you.' Without giving him time to reply, she stalked from the room.

The numbers had thinned considerably, her parents standing by the door as people said their farewells. Mirry was still inwardly quaking from Jay's latest attack, and to keep herself occupied she took the heavy tray from Martha and bore it away to the kitchen where the helpers had already started work. Not unnaturally, the sole topic of conversation was Jay Elphick, a discussion Mirry avoided by bustling backwards and forwards clearing up.

Soon there was only the family remaining—and Jay seeing the solicitor off. 'I'll be in touch when the audit's complete,' Mr Golding was saying. 'In the meantime you're at liberty to make use of the house as and when you like.'

'Oh, I do hope you'll move in soon, Jay,' Cathy Grey said warmly. 'It's high time we got to know you. Come round to dinner this evening. That's if you don't have to rush back to London...'

Mirry saw first puzzlement and then suspicion reflected in Jay's silver-grey eyes, and tensed for the snub she was sure was coming. At that moment he glanced at her, and as if in answer to her silent plea said with cool courtesy, 'Thank you, Mrs Grey, but as you say, I have other commitments.'

Her mother looked disappointed, but there was no lessening of her warmth. 'Some other time then, Jay, and soon. We're your family now, so you must feel free to drop in at the Dower House whenever you like.'

Mirry began to collect up the last of the glasses so she didn't hear Jay's reply. Her tray was overloaded and her father took it from her. Mirry removed three dangerously balanced glasses and followed him to the kitchen. As they were passing the open door of the library Mirry heard Annabel's voice say, 'You can't spend the evening alone here, Jay. Why not come back with us for a meal?'

Expecting Jay to give the same excuse he had offered her mother, she was stunned to hear him accept with real pleasure. So much for his 'other commitments', Mirry thought indignantly, exchanging glances with her father.

'I must say he's different from what I expected,' Sandra declared as they all walked back to the Dower House. 'Much more sophisticated.'

'A bit of a cold fish, I thought,' Richard commented.

'Annabel didn't think so,' Sandra pointed out with no thought for Andrew. 'She was all over him like a rash.

And you have to admit, he *is* attractive. Didn't you think so, Mirry?'

Glancing at Andrew's set expression, she declared loyally, 'Not as handsome as any of my brothers, and certainly not as nice.'

'Oh, you...' Sandra pouted.

Cathy Grey, well aware that her daughter-in-law had always been a little jealous of the closeness of the Greys, steered the topic into safer waters, not knowing that her regretful, 'Such a pity Jay had to rush back to London,' brought an indignant retort bubbling to Mirry's tongue.

But a warning shake of her father's head had Mirry biting back the words, and as the path narrowed he dropped back beside her, saying in an undertone, 'No sense in hurting your mother's feelings, pet.'

Mirry sighed her agreement, but her resentment hadn't quite died. 'Would you believe he's got some cock-eyed idea that we must resent him for inheriting Wenlow instead of one of us having it!'

Her father's left eyebrow shot upwards.

'Oh, I soon put him right,' Mirry dismissed, 'but he still seems... well, to bear our family a grudge.'

Donald was silent for several paces, staring thoughtfully at the ground. 'Human nature's a funny thing,' he said at last. 'At eighteen Jay might have decided to go it alone, but that wouldn't necessarily prevent him resenting the people who *have* been close to his father.'

'You mean he could be jealous of us, growing up here while he...'

'Something like that,' her father agreed. 'And you have to remember he was thrown in at the deep end today. It can't have been easy for him.'

'I suppose not,' Mirry said thoughtfully. 'What do you think we should do, Dad? Georgie was so keen for us to help him settle down here.'

'We'll go about our business as usual and do our best to draw Jay in, however much he kicks.' He grinned at his daughter's dubious expression. 'It won't be the first time your mother and I have come up against hostility—and overcome it. Some of your foster brothers and sisters were very antisocial when they first came to us.'

Mirry thought about what her father had said. Her parents might be able to turn the other cheek to Jay's hostility, but she wasn't sure she could. It was an unpleasant feeling to be disliked on sight, something that had never happened to her before.

Stripping off, she showered quickly and put on fresh underwear before dressing in a full black calf-length skirt printed with emerald-green flowers round the hem and a matching emerald-green shirt, cinching them together with a wide black belt.

Blessed with a fine, clear complexion that needed no more than a little moisturiser as protection from the wind, she brushed a bronze shadow on to her eyelids and found herself wishing she had the kind of looks that would make Jay smile at her the way he had smiled at Annabel.

'And if wishes were horses, pigs might fly,' she mocked her reflection, deciding there and then to follow her father's advice. Had she been a raving beauty it might have softened Jay's attitude towards her and her family, but she wasn't and never would be. She could only be her natural self and hope she could achieve results by sheer persistence. She grinned. Like water dripping on stone. Sweeping the mascara wand over her long lashes, she finished her perfunctory make-up with a browny-pink lipgloss. Pulling the pins out of her hair, she brushed it hard before catching the sides up on the crown of her head with a pretty slide and leaving the rest loose, and without bothering to glance in the mirror again she hurried downstairs.

The Greys were rarely all together under one roof, so there was more than enough to talk about over dinner, catching up on each other's news. After the meal was eaten and cleared away, most of the family were eager to attend this special meeting of the jazz club, taking the path beneath the trees that skirted the garden centre's nursery beds and approached the Hall from the back.

Like so much at Wenlow, the music-room's original opulence was a little faded now, the painted panels in the elaborate plasterwork ceiling in need of cleaning, the velvet upholstery on the gilt-legged chairs and sofas too worn to be sure what the original colour had been. But the polished oak floor had the patina of age and the grand piano was always kept in tune.

By the time they were ready to begin, the room was full to overflowing. The programme had been carefully chosen, every number with a reason for its inclusion, Abby Minto's arrangement of the Beatles' song 'Hey, Jude' because it had been one of Georgie's favourites. Closing her eyes as she coaxed the running, soaring notes out of the clarinet, Mirry liked to think Georgie's spirit was still around, listening.

After the applause had died down, Keir Minto got to his feet. 'We're here tonight to pay tribute to one very remarkable lady,' he said. 'A lady who showed us all by example how to take life by the throat and get the best possible out of it. If the last number was one of her favourites, the next one could be called her theme song. She always took the solo lead herself, but there's no one better qualified to assume her mantle than Mirry Grey.'

Mirry got to her feet, tears she was powerless to stem welling in her eyes. Letting them run unashamedly down her cheeks while she waited for Keir to give the lead-in to 'I Did It My Way', she poured all the emotion into the music, her slender body swaying, her long hair flying as she made the clarinet sob and sing.

There was laughter as well as applause as number followed number, especially when Simon took a turn on the double bass. Last but one, they played a blues which expressed the grief they all felt at losing a well-loved friend, but they finished with a triumphal 'When The Saints Go Marching In', the audience rising to their feet to join in, singing and clapping, and Mirry was easily able to imagine Georgie's delighted chuckle.

The audience surged around the players, offering their congratulations; Mirry, still on a high, sparkled back, accepting a can of lager and drinking thirstily.

She had her head tipped back as she heard Annabel enthuse, 'Mirry, you were fantastic! Wasn't she, Jay?'

Mirry lowered the can to meet Jay's cold, enigmatic gaze, and again she felt the half-painful, half-pleasurable jolt. Though Annabel was casually dressed she looked bandbox fresh, her hair swinging in a smooth bell to her shoulders, while Mirry felt hot and untidy.

'Indeed, extremely talented,' Jay agreed. 'Do you play professionally...er...Mirry?'

Her eyes widened. Was he actually paying her a compliment, or merely being sarcastic? 'No, only for the fun of it,' she said warily.

'But you're good enough to turn professional if you wanted to, Mirry,' Annabel claimed with genuine admiration. She turned a smiling face up to the man at her side. 'Are you musical, Jay?'

His poker face melted into real amusement. 'Efforts were made to teach me the piano, but with minimal success, so no, I can't claim to be musical.'

Taken off guard by his smile, Mirry said reminiscently, 'Your father wasn't, either. He couldn't carry a tune to save his life.'

She saw a smile freeze on Jay's face, but unaware that they were straying into a subject that was unwelcome to him, Annabel enlarged, 'He still came to all the jazz club meetings, didn't he, Mirry? And enjoyed them, too. But then Sir David and Lady Georgie always did everything together. Devoted to each other right to the end.' Only then did she suddenly remember she was talking to Sir David's illegitimate son, and her cheeks flooded with colour. 'I mean...I didn't... Oh, dear!'

To make matters worse, Andrew said pointedly, 'If Jay wants to know anything about David and Georgie, he should talk to Mirry. She knew them far better than you, Annabel.'

Mirry knew her brother's intervention had been prompted by his jealousy of the attention Annabel was paying Jay, but she wished he hadn't. She tried to head him off. 'People are beginning to leave, Andrew, so perhaps we could start straightening up...' She reached out to put her half-empty lager can on a side-table, missed the edge and gasped as the can fell to spill the remaining beer in a sticky pool on the polished floor. 'Oh, no! I'll get a cloth...'

Cheeks hot with mortification at her clumsiness, she hurried along the lengthy passageways to the kitchen. At least she had broken up an uncomfortable scene, but she wished she hadn't made quite such a fool of herself to do it.

The music-room had cleared considerably when she returned with the floor cloth, her brothers straightening up the chairs. Of Jay and Annabel there was no sign, though Andrew's glowering expression told her they had left together. She mopped up the mess she had made and, collecting the empty cans in a plastic bin-liner, returned them to the kitchen. Martha had long since gone to her quarters, but with the familiarity of long practice Mirry unlocked the back door and deposited the plastic bag by the dustbins before carefully locking it again and crossing to the sink to awash out the sticky floor cloth.

The Wenlow kitchen was even more enormous than the one at the Dower House, and as Mirry had switched on only one of the lights it was gloomy too, so, hearing a sudden sound behind her, she whirled round, her heart pumping in fright, to see Jay standing in the doorway.

'Oh! Oh, you did startle me!' she gasped.

'I startled *you*?' He surveyed her sardonically. 'The last thing I expected was to find the Little Miracle playing Cinderella in the kitchen.'

CHAPTER FOUR

IT SEEMED to Mirry she had blushed more today than in her whole life before. Hearing Jay use the full version of her nickname came as a shock, and the way he said it showed there was no lessening of his dislike.

He was still wearing the sleek grey business suit, but now his tie had been discarded and his collar was undone. Mirry couldn't seem to tear her gaze away from the strong column of his throat as he said, 'I assumed Mirry was short for Miranda until Mr Golding read out your real name. I was curious, so I asked Mrs Barks.'

Mirry cringed inwardly, for of course Martha would explain that, after Donald and Cathy had produced five sons, unexpectedly getting the little girl they had longed for had seemed like a miracle. The story had never bothered her before, but now, beneath Jay's silvery, sardonic gaze, it seemed embarrassingly sentimental.

'I suppose you find it stupid,' she said defensively, her small chin lifting, 'but as there was already a Catherine and a Georgina, it caused less confusion when Mirry stuck.'

'Ah, yes, Lady Georgina.' Jay pushed away from the door and moved slowly towards her, making Mirry's heart thump disturbingly. 'Your brother claims you knew her better than Annabel did, and my—Sir David. So do you subscribe to her theory of their mutual devotion?'

Mirry had noticed that stumble before, whenever Jay had spoken of David. Curiously she blurted, 'You never refer to him as your father, do you?'

Her question halted him a couple of feet away. 'It takes more than impregnating a woman to become a father,' he said curtly. 'And you didn't answer my question. Not that you need to when we both know that I'm the living proof that their so-called devoted marriage was a sham.'

'Oh, Jay...' Unaware that she was clutching the damp floor cloth to her chest, Mirry said earnestly, 'I don't expect you to find it easy to understand, but David and Georgie *did* share a deeply loving relationship all their lives. No...' she held up a hand as he would have made an angry denial '... I'm not glossing over David's affair with your mother, but in the circumstances... Well, let's just say Georgie was able to understand and forgive.'

'It was so important to her to be Lady Jayston?' he sneered, and if Mirry thought those grey eyes cold before it was nothing to the frost in them now.

She shook her head vehemently. 'As if that mattered to her! In fact, she offered David a divorce at the time. She knew she could never give him the children he wanted, you see, and she loved him enough to give him the chance of a family with someone else. And it says a lot for the strength of David's love that he begged her not to leave him. Because he *did* want you, Jay. He wanted you enough to plead with your mother to allow him to adopt you, and when she refused, to go on hoping for years that she might change her mind.' The strength of her emotion brought tears to her eyes, and she could only see Jay through a haze.

But both his sneering tone and his words told her she hadn't convinced him. 'So that's the line you Greys are taking! Such a touching story, too, so tell me, if my father wanted me so much, why did he rarely make the effort to see me? Never more than a few times a year, and then only for an hour or two. Not that I wanted to see him at all.' For the first time there was a ring of real emotion instead of the sneering distaste. 'God, those are the worst memories of my childhood, dressed in my best clothes and threatened to be on my best behaviour...'

'But, Jay...' Mirry's heart was wrung for the bewildered, hurt small boy he had once been. 'That wasn't your father's doing. It was your mother who rationed the visits.'

'Well, of course, you *would* blame my mother.' Jay's lips curled contemptuously. 'The Greys made mischief then, and it seems they're still bent on making it.'

Mirry's eyes widened. 'What do you mean, the Greys made mischief?'

'They didn't mention that when they fed you that heart-wrenching saga?' His eyebrows rose in mock surprise. 'The way your parents raked up old scandals about my mother? Told David downright lies to blacken her character, like suggesting some other man was responsible for her pregnancy?' His mouth thinned to a grim line while his eyes took on the blankness of the inward-looking. 'If there was one thing my mother was most consistent about it was her bitterness over the way Donald and Cathy Grey split her and David up in their determination to hang on to their corner of Wenlow.'

For just a few moments a little worm of doubt crept into Mirry's mind: not that her parents had interfered because they feared to lose the Dower House and garden

centre, but when she remembered how forceful her
mother had been in her opinion of Valerie Elphick, it
was quite possible that they *had* pressured David into
standing by his wife. It was only natural that their sym-
pathies would be with Georgie.

As if sensing Mirry was no longer so sure of herself,
Jay pressed home his attack. 'And if the allegedly so
concerned Sir David Jayston was really so keen to acknowledge the product of his liaison—according to you
to the lengths of wanting to adopt me—then how come
he never provided a penny piece towards my support?'

Mirry was too taken aback to do anything but gape
at him, and as if relishing her speechlessness Jay went
on, 'All right, so my mother was a comparatively wealthy
woman, but that fact runs a coach and horses through
your cosy little theory, wouldn't you say?'

At last Mirry managed to close her mouth. 'But that's
just not true! David always supported both you and
Valerie, right up to the time you finished university.
Before you were born he sold the Dower House to my
father and settled the money on your mother. And since
then there have been other sales—Dicken's Farm, Odden
Wood. That's why the estate's in such a bad way now.
It's a downright lie to suggest your father didn't take his
responsibility towards you seriously.' Indignation was
nearly shooting flames through the top of her skull, and
it occurred to her that, if Valerie had lied to Jay about
this, she might also have lied to him about her parents'
responsibility in breaking up David's affair.

But if Mirry was close to losing her temper, Jay was
suddenly very cool. 'How old did you say you were?'

She blinked, the seemingly irrelevant question taking some of the steam out of her. 'Twenty-three, but what's that——'

'So how do you come to be such an expert on what happened thirty years ago?' he asked with steely logic. 'The way you tell it, you might have watched it happen. But it's only hearsay, isn't it?' He took a deep breath, releasing the air from his lungs in a hissing, 'Whereas I *lived* through it.'

Mirry was silenced, conceding that he had every justification for disbelieving her view of the events. It *was* all second-hand knowledge, passed on by Georgie and by her mother, both of whom were admittedly prejudiced on the subject of Valerie Elphick. And yet the close, loving partnership that had been David and Georgie's marriage was not hearsay. That was something she had observed for herself. And Jay's allegation that his father had made no contribution towards his maintenance was certainly untrue.

She shivered as a feeling of clammy coldness crept over her, only then discovering she had been hugging the damp floor cloth all this time. She tossed it into the sink, saying quietly to Jay, 'I don't pretend to be an expert on something that happened before I was born. There's no way I can prove to you that your father's marriage was a good one, or that both he and Georgie would have given anything for you to have shared in their closeness. But there is something *you* can prove.'

Jay didn't appear to be listening. His eyes were riveted on her breasts, and when she glanced down she saw to her consternation the dampness had spread to the material of her shirt, moulding it lovingly to her outline. And shockingly her nipples sprang to attention beneath his gaze, proclaiming the disturbing effect he was having on her.

'And what can I prove?' He sounded barely interested, but the fact that he had after all been listening even while watching her body's response to him was somehow even more humiliating.

Snatching the material away from her skin with both hands, she said, ashamed of the quaver in her voice, 'That your mother wasn't telling the truth when she claimed your father didn't support you. The estate records will show the properties that had to be sold, and Mr Golding can tell you exactly where the money went.'

'And why should I bother?' Jay dismissed.

His indifference caught her on the raw, and she snapped angrily, 'Because when you find your mother lied to you about that, you might begin to wonder if she lied about other things. Your father not wanting you, for one.' Her chin lifted challengingly. 'Or are you afraid?'

'My God! You're like a mosquito.' The façade of indifference cracked to show a very angry man. 'What does it take to shut you up? This?' His hands snaked out to grasp her shoulders, almost lifting her off her feet and slamming her against his chest. The breath left her lungs with an audible gasp, and before she could draw another his mouth drove down on hers. He was angry and meant to hurt, and succeeded too as shock left her unresisting, her brain reeling.

Then she was free, able to drag breath back into her starved lungs. Her shocked gaze locked with his, her shaking hand lifting to her bruised mouth. For a fleeting moment his eyes held what might have been compunction, but then it froze over as he ground out, 'I think you'd better get out of here before I do something else I'll regret. And if you know what's good for you, you'll keep out.'

Mirry backed a couple of paces as if from a wild beast it would be dangerous to turn her back on, then, whirling, she took to her heels.

The thud of hoofs on the grass, the jingle of harness and creak of saddle leather, and above all the unalloyed joy on the face of the little Down's Syndrome girl perched on the pony's back had Mirry's spirits back to their normal level for the first time in days.

As part of his remedial therapy, Nick had been put back on a horse. At first Mirry had been in an agony of apprehension, afraid even a minor tumble would undo all the work they had put in to rehabilitate him. But, under George Frost's expert guidance in the beginners' paddock at the riding stables, Nick's confidence had slowly returned as he relearned all his old skills. And the obvious benefits had prompted George Frost into contacting a local organisation for the physically and mentally handicapped and arranging two weekly sessions for their members. Grateful to George for all he had done for Nick, Mirry had volunteered to be one of his helpers.

Not only did it give the young riders enjoyment and a new confidence, it gave the city children a taste of the countryside, where the changing seasons always meant something new to look out for. Now the pussy willows along the stream wore their fat catkins, and across the stream in Odden Wood came the fast, vibrating drumming of a woodpecker.

But Odden Wood reminded Mirry of her argument with Jay, his towering rage and devastating kiss. That was more than a week ago now, and she had tried hard to put it out of her mind, only to have the memory return again and again. She'd tried telling herself it had been more of an assault than a kiss, but that hadn't stopped the blood stirring hotly in her veins. Jay had been very explicit, demonstrating his anger and his dislike, yet it was as if her body had picked up different signals and was reacting independently.

When the lesson was over, Annabel called, 'Hi, Mirry. Got time to help me rub down? Dad's got to rush off to deliver a colt to his new home.'

'Sure.' Leading the pony into the stable, she began to unsaddle. 'How's the stud side going?'

'Pretty good. We'll never breed a Derby winner, but Dad's got several good hunters coming along, and there's a young horse that could make a champion show-jumper in the right hands. As a matter of fact...' Annabel began to rub down the pony '...Jay was very interested in him.'

Mirry's head jerked up. '*Jay* was? He does ride, then?' That would be something else Jay and Annabel would have in common.

'Not for himself! He says all he knows about horses are that they have a leg at each corner.' Her giggle invited Mirry to share the joke. 'But he knows a girl who's looking for a horse, the daughter of some business colleague who has ambitions in the show ring.'

'Oh.' Mirry couldn't help being pleased Jay didn't ride, then felt ashamed of such an unworthy reaction. To punish herself she said, 'You've been seeing a fair bit of Jay. Has he told you anything of his plans?'

Annabel shook her head. 'He's been pretty cagey, but I don't think there's much doubt that he'll sell Wenlow.'

'Sell?' Mirry's shock startled the pony who sidestepped.

'Yes, more's the pity. There aren't that many attractive men around here for a girl to romance with.' Annabel tossed her head a shade defensively, as if she knew Mirry was thinking of Andrew. 'Oh, he hasn't said it in as many words, but before he went back to London he let slip that when he came back he'd be bringing some businessmen to look over the place. Anyway...' she straightened to face Mirry over the pony's back '...whatever his plans, he won't make a decision overnight, so he'll be around for a while yet.'

If Mirry had comforted herself that Annabel's flirtation with Jay was merely to turn the screw on Andrew, the look of excited anticipation on the other girl's face gave the lie to that theory. It was a look that said Annabel was savouring special memories. Jay's kisses? Well, of course he would have kissed her. Kisses that would be nothing like the assault with which he had punished Mirry Grey! She was dismayed at the actual physical pain this caused her. Nothing remotely like it had ever happened to her before, but she had no trouble in identifying it as jealousy.

And that was a destructive emotion. Just because she had discovered what it was like to be intensely attracted to a man, it was no justification for feeling hurt and betrayed because he was feeling a similar violent attraction for another woman. It wasn't going to be easy, watching as Annabel and Jay fell in love, but there had been a Jayston at Wenlow for nearly five hundred years and she couldn't see the tradition broken now, when it

was possible she could do something about it. 'Aunt
Georgie was worried that Jay might not be able to afford
to keep the Hall,' she said slowly. 'That's why she came
up with this scheme...'

'Scheme? What scheme?' Annabel demanded.

Mirry explained Georgie's idea of turning the wings
of the house into self-contained flats in order to give Jay
extra income, and about the plans Mirry herself had
drawn up.

'What did Jay say when you told him?' Annabel asked,
and Mirry had to admit she hadn't told him yet.

'Why ever not?' Annabel was incredulous. 'Oh, Mirry,
you *must*. It could make all the difference. Look, as
soon as he comes back, show them to him. Please...'

Mirry avoided her pleading gaze. 'It's not as easy as
that. In the first place, all the copies are up at the Hall,
and in the second place... well, you must have noticed
Jay and I don't get on too well.'

A rather odd expression crossed Annabel's face,
pleased yet curious. 'You don't like him?'

'*He* doesn't like *me*,' Mirry corrected.

'But this is much too important to let a clash of
temperament get in the way,' the other girl pleaded. 'At
least tell him he does have an alternative to selling. He'd
be very grateful.'

As she drove home Mirry wondered what she had let
herself in for. What would Jay's reaction be when she
showed him the plans? One thing she was sure of: Jay
wouldn't fall on her neck with gratitude as Annabel had
implied.

Hot and sticky, she made straight for her room to strip
off the jeans and shirt that smelled faintly of horse.
Lingering beneath the shower, she pondered her prob-

lem, and by the time she was dressing again in a soft turquoise skirt and sweater, she had made up her mind.

It was the coward's way out, to find the plans and leave them where Jay couldn't avoid seeing them, together with an explanatory letter. And what better time to do it than now, while Jay was safely in London?

She kept the explanation to a minimum, just stating the facts: that Lady Jayston had had the plans drawn up in order to provide Jay with sufficient income to allow him to live at Wenlow, that there should be enough funds in Georgie's personal bequest to cover the cost, but that the plans had yet to be submitted to the local council. Sealing the letter, she wrote Jay's name clearly on the front and took it with her as she slipped out of the house, using the well-worn path between the two properties and letting herself into the Hall by the kitchen door.

A harrassed Martha turned from the kitchen table where she was rolling out pastry. 'Less than two hours' notice!' she burst out. 'I wouldn't mind, but there's three extra bedrooms to get ready, as well as the cooking.'

'You mean Jay's here now?' Mirry retreated a couple of steps.

'Heaven forbid! Nancy's only just gone up to see to the bedrooms. And what I'd have done if she *hadn't* been willing to drop everything and come I *don't* know.' Martha bad-temperedly folded over the flaky pastry and slapped it down again on the table. 'Didn't even have the courtesy to tell me himself. Left it to some secretary to phone me. No consideration.'

'If there's anything I can do...' Mirry volunteered unthinkingly.

'And have his lordship say I'm past it? Fine London folk! I've cooked for better quality than them, and so

I told that young woman.' For all her truculence, Mirry could see the hands wielding the rolling pin had not lost their light touch.

'That's right, Martha, you show 'em,' she said mischievously.

'That I shall!' But Martha's eyes were beginning to twinkle. 'Don't mind me, love. Does a body good to have a good grumble. What was it you wanted?'

'Nothing that need hinder you, Martha,' she assured the housekeeper. 'I just want to look out those conversion plans and leave them for Mr Elphick. I've got a letter that'll explain.'

'Well, you know where they are better than I do.' Martha went back to rolling her pastry.

The trouble was, Mirry didn't know where Georgie had put them. The logical place would be the bureau in her sitting-room, but a thorough search revealed only her godmother's correspondence. Perhaps they were in the library; Georgie had sometimes used the desk in there.

Hurrying downstairs again, Mirry had the uneasy feeling of a trespasser, but she pushed on into the library. The desk there was much larger, with twice the number of drawers. Beginning at the top, she worked systematically downwards. Some of them were empty where Mr Golding had removed the estate books for auditing, other's still held papers, but not the ones she was looking for.

The last drawer was stiff, coming a little way out and then jamming. Mirry had to get down on her hands and knees to ease it, and then it finally came with a rush, tipping her backwards, the corner pecking a lump out of her shin while her head banged painfully against the metal base of the chair.

'What the hell!'

Hugging her shin and still dazed from the blow to her head, Mirry gazed up at an all too familiar figure looming over the top of the desk. 'Oh, God!' she said in a strangled voice and closed her eyes to shut him out.

'You might well say your prayers,' Jay said with menacing softness. 'Going in for a bit of petty larceny, Miss Grey?'

'N-no.' Pushing the drawer and its scattered contents out of the way, Mirry scrambled groggily to her feet. That was when she saw the three very interested spectators behind Jay, two men and a young girl. Three witnesses to her humiliation.

CHAPTER FIVE

MIRRY took a deep breath and tried to summon her scattered wits sufficiently to make the explanation they were all obviously waiting for. 'I-I'm sorry. I know this must look...but I'd hoped to find them and leave them out and be gone by the time you got here,' she babbled.

'I'm sure you did,' Jay said coldly. 'Mean to be gone before I got here anyway, though I doubt you meant to leave behind whatever it is you're searching for.'

Mirry's face whitened. He was as good as calling her a thief! And if everyone had their rights, those plans were still *her* property. 'Oh, I know in your opinion there's nothing too low for a Grey to stoop to,' she burst out bitterly. 'But in fact I was trying to do you a favour. Hah! I warned Annabel you——'

'Annabel?' Jay broke in sharply. 'What does your snooping here have to do with Annabel?'

Snooping! It took all Mirry's self-control to contain her rage. She managed it as she said tightly, 'Annabel wished you to know you had an alternative to selling,' but some of it spilled out as she went on, 'For some odd reason, she would like you to stay on here at Wenlow. Personally I'd just as soon you sold up and went.'

She might have known her lie would backfire on her. Jay's left eyebrow rose sardonically. 'Honesty at last, Miss Grey? All right, I'll buy it. What is this alternative Annabel wishes me to know about?'

Mirry had left her explanatory letter on top of the desk when she began her search. Now she pushed it across towards Jay. 'It's all in there,' she said abruptly, taking care to avoid contact as he reached to take it.

Reaction was beginning to set in; all she wanted to do was sit down and howl as Jay ripped open the envelope and scanned the contents, but not for anything would she display her weakness.

As she bent to pick up the loose drawer and ram it back into place, one of the men still hovering in the doorway said, 'Perhaps you'd prefer to sort this out in private, Jay,' reminding Mirry of the audience she had forgotten.

She straightened quickly saying, 'There's no need, I'm leaving myself now.' But as she came out from behind the desk she began to feel most peculiar, the floor moving up and down beneath her feet. She reached for a chair, clutching the back of it while she took several deep breaths to try to steady herself. From a long way away she heard a girlish voice say, 'Oh, you've hurt your leg. It's bleeding!' And, through the gathering darkness a male voice, 'She's going to faint!' Seconds later she was being lifted into the chair, her head pushed down to her knees while the same voice demanded, 'A drop of brandy, Jay.'

Mirry tried to protest that she was all right, but her tongue felt too big for her mouth, then a glass was pressed to her lips. The impulse to swallow was automatic, and she gasped for breath as the fiery spirit hit the back of her throat. But though it made her gag and brought tears to her eyes, at least it cleared her head.

'I think you should put a plaster on that cut.' The girl, who could be no more than sixteen, was kneeling on the floor beside her chair, and Mirry looked down to see the jagged hole in her tights and blood oozing from the gash in her shin.

'It's all right,' she dismissed, uncomfortable to find herself the unwilling centre of attention. 'I'll see to it when I get home.'

'You'll see to it now,' Jay said in a voice that brooked no argument. 'Do you know where there's a first-aid box?'

'There's one in Aunt Georgie's bathroom,' Mirry said. 'But really, you needn't——'

But he was already pulling her to her feet and saying, 'Pour Alan a drink, Philip, and there's ginger ale for Tricia. I won't be long.' And Mirry found herself being swept from the room and up the stairs. 'Which way?' he said as they reached the top.

Mirry indicated with one hand. Opening the door to the sitting-room, she asked curiously, 'Haven't you looked round the house yet?'

'Parts of it.' Then, abruptly changing the subject, he asked, 'So where are those architect's plans you wanted me to know about?'

'If I knew, I'd have left them with the letter and got out of here before you arrived,' Mirry retorted. 'I thought they'd be in there...' she indicated the little bureau '...and when they weren't I tried downstairs.'

'You'd better see to your leg.' Again the abrupt change of subject. Mirry sighed, deciding that, the sooner she did as he wanted, the sooner he'd allow her to leave.

In the bathroom she stripped off her torn tights, bathed the wound with antiseptic and stuck an adhesive plaster over it, then returned to the sitting-room where

she found Jay by the bookcase. 'They won't be there,'
she said. 'They're rolled up and——'

'I *do* know what architect's plans look like,' he said
curtly, his gaze falling to the pink plaster now adorning
her shapely leg. 'You're feeling better?'

'I'm fine.' Mirry's expressive face proclaimed her
awareness that he didn't care either way.

'So if they're not here, and not in the library, where
else are they likely to be?' Jay demanded. 'That's if they
really exist at all.'

Would he ever speak to her without that jeering challenge? Mirry wondered. It was on the tip of her tongue
to retort that she had drawn them up herself, but she
realised if Jay knew *that*, he would be even more
prejudiced against the idea. 'Georgie had them the day
before she died,' she said quietly. 'She intended to post
them to the local council the following morning, only
she——' Her voice wobbled as a wave of grief bowled
her over. Turning away from Jay until the wave ebbed
and she could trust her voice again, she eventually managed, 'That's why I was surprised not to find them in
here. I don't know... Perhaps Helen knows where they
are!'

'Helen?' Jay asked blankly.

'Helen Dutton. Aunt Georgie's nurse. In fact, I could
ring her...' Mirry's hand reached towards the extension
phone, then hesitated. 'With your permission?' At his
curt acquiescence she dialled the number.

Mirry looked at Jay as she put the phone down after
the short conversation. 'In the bedroom. Helen said she
put them away herself.' Walking through to the adjoining
room, she circled the big double bed David and Georgie
had shared for thirty-five years, its faded elegance marred
by the metal bed lift.

Reaching the night-table, Mirry slid open the drawer and took out the dozen or so tightly rolled sheets of stiff paper. 'Here they are.' She held the bundle out to him. 'May I go now?'

But Jay was staring at the metal contraption over the bed, his eyes drawn back to it again after giving the rolled plans only a flicking glance as he took them from her. 'I didn't know my—my father was bedridden before he died.'

'Your *father*! Of course he wasn't.' Already moving towards the door, Mirry looked back at him curiously. Didn't he know? Obviously not, from the shaken look on his face. 'The bed lift was Georgie's. Not that she was bedridden by a long way. That was hers, too.' She pointed at the electric wheelchair still standing in the corner. 'I'm not sure if that's mark seven or mark eight. She was pretty hard on her wheelchairs, taking them into places other people would hesitate to try, but then, after thirty-three years of managing them she was pretty experienced. Georgie had a riding accident just two years after she was married and broke her back,' she added softly as he turned his stunned gaze on her.

'Thirty-three years! But that means——'

'That she'd already been tied to a wheelchair for three years by the time you were born,' Mirry finished for him. 'Odd that your mother never mentioned that fact when she was telling you the "true" version of the story.' She walked out, leaving Jay staring after her.

Annabel phoned later that evening. 'Mirry? Jay's back. He's bringing the Charlesworth girl round to look at that horse tomorrow, but he never mentioned anything about

his plans for the Hall and I didn't like to ask. Did
you——?'

'I think you can safely say they've been brought to
his notice,' Mirry said with wry understatement. Not for
anything did she want to go into details of the humiliating position she'd found herself in with Jay, but
Annabel was too busying pouring out her thanks to ask
questions.

The poor girl had really got it bad, Mirry thought
wryly. And why not, when Mirry herself had felt the
pull of Jay's attraction? But that was something she had
to put out of her mind. She'd done all she could, now
it was up to Annabel to persuade him his inheritance
was worth holding on to.

The sun was surprisingly hot for April, and as there had
been no rain for more than a week the grass was quite
dry once the dew was off. Simon was still at home, and
where Simon was, things happened. Now he was driving
the mower round the tennis courts with all the enthusiasm of a small boy.

Years ago Aunt Georgie had had the idea of converting the Hall vegetable garden into a couple of grass
courts. Donald Grey had laid them and they were still
maintained—as were all the lawns at Wenlow—by the
garden centre. At breakfast that Saturday morning
Simon had reminded them there were likely to be people
round, hoping for a game.

Georgie had always encouraged everyone in the small
Wenlow community to use the courts, so in the past it
had functioned like a small private club. Mirry was the
only one to feel uneasy about Jay's reaction at discovering the local inhabitants making free with his

property, but when she had voiced her doubts they had all stared at her with expressions ranging from mild curiosity to downright amazement.

'Why the hell wouldn't he want his tennis courts prepared?' Andrew had demanded truculently. 'He seems to expect everything else to fall into his lap.'

'I did discuss it with him, Mirry,' her father said quietly. 'He said he'd be grateful if we'd continue to look after the garden, at least till everything's settled.'

Mirry found herself wondering when her father had seen Jay, what the atmosphere had been like, and whether Jay's antagonism had been in evidence. But she couldn't ask because she hadn't mentioned the further clashes she'd had with him.

Knowing he would be at the riding stables, Mirry was able to relax and enjoy her brothers' company. As Simon finished the first court she began to mark the white lines while Nick emptied the grass cuttings into the waiting trailer. The mowing finished, Simon erected the posts, then, while Mirry and Nick finished marking the second court, started an inspection of the surrounding wire netting fence.

'There's a break here,' he called after a while. 'I'll get some wire. Leave the nets till I get back, Mirry.'

She raised her hand in acknowledgement as he loped off, but when she'd finished marking the lines and he still wasn't back, she became impatient. Leaving Nick cleaning the marking machine at the tap, she went into the little pavilion where all the kit was stored.

The nets had been rolled neatly at the end of last season and lay side by side on the wooden floor like a challenge. Dragging one of them across the floor to the top of the three shallow steps, she squatted down and managed to hoist it on to her shoulder. She was carefully straightening up when a roar from Simon made her stagger and she might have fallen if Nick hadn't grabbed her from behind.

'I thought I told you to leave the nets, you goof!' Simon scolded, hefting the burden from her and allowing her buckling knees to straighten.

'I could have done it if you hadn't startled me,' Mirry complained breathlessly. 'You know I'm——'

'—stronger than you look.' Simon grinned at her, then remarked over the top of her tousled head, 'What would you do with a sister like this, Jay? She refuses to take account of the fact she's a foot shorter and only half the weight of us.'

Mirry's head jerked round. She had taken it for granted it was Nick who had steadied her, but she found herself staring at Jay Elphick. This morning he was wearing well-cut cavalry twills and a thin cotton sweater in shades of fawn and grey that revealed a much more muscular build than his formal clothes had done. Even more astonishing, the ice in his silvery eyes had melted and he was looking amused.

'As I've never had one, the problem's outside my experience.'

Mirry didn't know what had caused the thaw in the ice, but she responded to it with a cheeky grin. 'Wouldn't you know it! *Another* male asserting his superiority! OK, I concede you are both superior——' she saw the two men exchange triumphant grins and added '—in the *brawn* depart.ment. So if you two strong men will carry the nets to the court, I'll get on with the more intellectually taxing job of stringing them up.'

'All right, bossy boots.' Simon hefted the net he was holding into the surprised Jay's arms and bounded into the pavilion to fetch the other. 'But don't think you're getting away with your cheek, young Mirry. Retribution will come!'

'You don't frighten me, Simon Grey,' Mirry jeered saucily, dancing ahead of them.

'When I first saw these courts I didn't think they'd been used for years,' Jay said when everything was done.

'Don't you believe it!' Simon grinned. 'David and Georgie were keen players.'

Jay looked at Mirry sharply. 'I thought you said your—that Lady Jayston was confined to a wheelchair.'

The thaw hadn't lasted long, Mirry thought wryly.

'Oh, Georgie never let a little thing like that stop her,' Simon answered for her. 'There wasn't much she couldn't do from that chair of hers. Do you play, Jay?'

Jay was looking bemused, as if the idea of anyone playing tennis from a wheelchair was beyond his comprehension. 'Er...no. At least, not since I was at university. Squash is my game.'

'Well, nobody's going to mind if you're rusty,' Simon assured him. 'We're a mixed bunch, from raw beginners to an ex-county player. Georgie encouraged everyone in the district to join in.'

Mirry thought it would be the best thing that could happen, that Jay should be made to feel part of their little community, but having been slapped down by him several times she was afraid he would feel the Greys were taking too much for granted again. 'Maybe Jay doesn't like the idea of having his tennis courts taken over every fine weekend, Simon,' she suggested warily.

Expecting Jay to agree with her, she was surprised when, after a few seconds' silence, he said casually, 'I've no objections to letting present arrangements stand...at least until I've decided what I'm going to do about the house.'

Mirry wanted to ask him whether he had studied the conversion plans and if he was considering that alternative, but Simon was slapping him on the shoulder. 'They're a grand bunch; some very pretty girls, too. And you'll have already met most of them. See you down here this afternoon, then, Jay.'

Mirry was accustomed to Simon's propensity for organising everyone and felt obliged to remind him, 'Jay does have house guests this weekend, Simon.'

'Well, bring them along, too,' he retorted cheerfully.

'And you call *me* bossy!' Mirry jeered, laughing.

'And so you are. *I'm* just displaying leadership qualities.' Simon grinned unrepentantly. 'And that reminds me...' Pouncing, he swept a squealing Mirry into his arms and dumped her into the trailer full of grass cuttings. She surfaced to find Nick joining in the fun, ready with a handful of grass to stuff down her neck. Squirming away, she picked up handfuls herself and hurled them at him; then, while she was picking grass out of her mouth and shaking it out of her hair, Simon started the little tractor and moved off, jerking her on to her back again. By the time she had righted herself they were well down the path, but looking back she saw Jay still standing there, a bemused expression on his face.

There was a good turn-out on the courts that afternoon. A spring weekend being a busy time for the garden centre, Andrew had been unable to join them, and as weekends were busy at the riding stables too,

Mirry didn't expect Annabel to be there either, but she was. Mirry couldn't help wondering if it was at Jay's express invitation or if she had come in the hopes of seeing him, though Jay himself hadn't as yet put in an appearance.

It was more than an hour later, when she came off court after a hard-fought game partnering Keir Minto against Simon and Annabel that she discovered Jay had arrived, he and his three guests clustering round Abigail's lounger. To her surprise the men greeted Keir like an old friend, and it was he who introduced Mirry while Jay congratulated Simon and Annabel on their narrow victory.

'Alan Charlesworth and his daughter Tricia, and Philip Amis. And this little firecracker is Mirry Grey. I fitted out their hotel chain with its computer system,' Keir went on to explain. 'Alpha Hotels.' Mirry recognised the name. 'So I'd met Alan and Philip many times before, though not Jay.'

'You mean...Jay works for Alpha Hotels?' Mirry asked, her eyes immediately going to Jay, only to find him watching her.

'Our financial director,' Philip Amis affirmed. 'We were lucky to get him.'

So much for her sister-in-law Sandra's patronising remark about the new heir being an impecunious bank clerk!

'We sort of met Miss Grey yesterday evening,' Alan Charlesworth said, smiling, 'though Jay's usually impeccable manners let him down and he didn't get round to an introduction.'

Mirry's cheeks burned at the reminder of Jay's accusation of snooping, but the twinkle in the man's eyes seemed to say the accusation had carried no weight with him. Keir was looking curious, but the last thing Mirry wanted was to have to explain, so she was grateful when his daughter asked, 'Your leg, Miss Grey? Is it OK now?'

'Fine, thanks.' She displayed the shin which still bore a bruise and a healing cut. She was aware of the eyes of the whole group on her, especially Jay's, and to counteract the discomfort this gave her she concentrated her attention on the young girl. 'And please call me Mirry. I tend to look around for someone else when anyone calls me Miss Grey. Would you like a game, Tricia?'

The girl's glance slid sideways to Nick, who was sitting on the grass. 'Well...I don't have a racquet, and anyway I'm nowhere near as good as the rest of you.'

'No problem. There's a racquet.' Mirry handed the girl her own. 'And Nick'll be only too happy to have a game with someone who won't run him off his feet. He's not back to form yet after his accident.' She spoke casually but watched the girl's reaction, pleased at Tricia's unconcealed eagerness at the suggestion, even more pleased that, though Nick's scramble to his feet was less than athletic, he was taking care to speak slowly and distinctly as he led Tricia on to the court.

Once again Mirry felt she was being watched, and glancing across saw the four men talking earnestly. At least, three of them were; although Jay appeared to be listening, his enigmatic grey eyes captured hers across the space.

'Business!' Abby said disgustedly. 'I suppose I'll have it all evening too. Jay's bringing his guests to me for dinner.' She brightened. 'You wouldn't do me a favour and come along, too, Mirry? If anyone's guaranteed to take their minds off perpetual business...'

'Me?' Mirry glanced involuntarily at Jay, but this time his attention was centred on Annabel. 'If you want your evening to be a success you'll have to count me out, Abby. I'm the last person Jay would want to see.'

Abby's eyebrows soared. 'I know you claim he disliked you on sight, but——'

'And since then his opinion has sunk even lower,' Mirry assured her friend.

'Oh, come on, Mirry.' Abby was openly disbelieving. 'If he dislikes you so much, how come he's hardly taken his eyes off you since he got here?'

'Probably to give himself time to take avoiding action if I get too close,' she retorted promptly. 'Honestly, Abby, if you really want to please Jay, then you'll ask Annabel to partner him.'

'She does seem to have fallen for him, doesn't she?' Abby said thoughtfully. 'Funny, I would have laid bets that she intended to forgive Andrew soon. But talking of partners, I'm still going to be one man heavy, so there's no reason why both you *and* Annabel can't come.'

If there was one thing Mirry liked the idea of less than being thrust upon Jay, it was having to spend the evening watching him with Annabel. 'I still don't think it's a good idea,' she said firmly. 'If he made one of his snide remarks, I'm quite likely to fire a rocket at him, and that could be embarrassing for everyone. Besides, it's Simon's last night.'

'Oh, well, if you won't, you won't.' Abby sighed regretfully. 'I still think it's a pity. Jay has a brilliant brain, and from what I've seen, a computer for a heart. Yet have you noticed his mouth?'

Mirry stared at her. 'I've noticed it's the one feature he's inherited from David . . . except that Jay keeps his sort of buttoned up.'

'Exactly!' Abby leaned forward confidentially. 'The mouth of a sensualist if ever I saw one, yet he keeps all that buttoned up along with his emotions. I've nothing against Annabel, but she'll never strike sparks off him like you will, Mirry. And that's what Jay needs, someone to wake him up and show him he's alive.'

Before Mirry could think of a reply, Keir dropped on to his haunches on the other side of the lounger. 'OK, honey?' Startled, both girls looked up to see Jay and Annabel standing right behind him, and, wondering if any of them had overheard, they flushed guiltily.

Abby recovered first. 'Annabel, Jay's bringing his guests along for dinner with us tonight. I know it's short notice, but you will be able to join us, won't you?'

'Why, thank you, I'd love to,' Annabel accepted breathlessly with a sidelong glance at Jay.

'I had hoped Mirry would come along too,' Abby went on guilelessly, 'but she turned me down.'

Mirry could feel Jay's eyes boring into her, and though she tried hard to resist her own glance was drawn to him. He was angry, the clenched jaw and fiercely silver eyes betrayed it. Yet why? Certainly not because she had turned the invitation down. Maybe it was because Abby had asked her at all, thereby laying him open to the risk of having to spend time in her company. The thought was so depressing, she jumped to her feet and offered herself to make up the next foursome.

CHAPTER SIX

THE DOWER HOUSE rang with young voices that evening. Many of Simon's friends had descended on them to make the most of this last opportunity before he returned to London. Tricia Charlesworth, too, had begged to be excused from an evening spent with adults in favour of Nick's invitation, leaving Abby's dinner-table even more overbalanced with males.

Mirry was delighted to see the way Nick responded to Tricia's interest. If he got a bit excited and slurred his speech, she showed no embarrassment, and when Simon put on a pile of records for dancing she pooh-poohed Nick's diffidence and actually persuaded him on to the floor with her. And already Mirry had overheard them making a date to go riding together in the morning. It was just what Nick needed, she decided, a pretty girl who could see beyond his handicaps to the handsome young man he was.

But although Mirry danced herself, and talked and laughed enough to fool anyone, half her mind was on Abby's dinner-table, imagining Annabel blossoming under Jay's attention.

At least her energetic day made her tired enough to fall asleep eventually, and if she still felt a little jaded the next morning she wasn't the only one. Simon arrived at the breakfast-table only minutes after Mirry, with a face as long as a camel's. The girl he had taken home after the party lived on an outlying farm, and, taking what should have been a short cut along a narrow track, he'd discovered too late someone had used the track as a rubbish dump. He'd run over an old bicycle which had cut one of the tyres of his prized Lotus to ribbons.

'I managed to change the wheel, but the spare's only an emergency wheel, not meant to do a hundred miles of motorway, and there's no hope of getting a new tyre fitted around here on a Sunday.' Simon dragged his hands frustratedly through his hair. 'I've *got* to get back on duty this afternoon. After all this leave there's no excuse for being late.'

'You could take my car,' his mother offered, though in rather a doubtful voice. Her runabout was an elderly Mini that was used to being coaxed along.

Not surprisingly, Simon grimaced. 'Thanks, Mum, but I don't think I'll risk it. I could be even worse off if the thing disintegrates on the motorway.'

'There's the estate car,' their father suggested. 'I reckon I can manage without it, provided you get it back here for next weekend.'

Simon shook his head hopelessly. 'I'm on long haul now, so it'll be at least ten days before I'm back in London.'

'There's no way we can manage without the truck or the Range Rover even for a day,' Andrew put in apologetically. 'So that only leaves the train.'

'And we all know what the Sunday service is like!' Simon groaned. 'I don't suppose you've got a timetable?'

Cathy shook her head. 'No, but Martha has. She uses the train to visit her sister in Bedford. Simon, wait... What about Jay's guests? They'll almost certainly be going back to London today, and one of them might be willing to give you a lift.'

'Mum, you're a genius!' Simon veered into the hall to the phone. A few minutes later he was back, beaming. 'It's all right. The Charlesworths are staying on to have lunch with the Frosts while they discuss the transportation of the horse they're buying, but Jay and Philip are going back to London later this morning.'

'That's solved your problem of getting back today,' Mirry said, wondering how Jay had received her brother's request. 'But how are you going to get your car back to London?'

'Ah, that's where having a sweet, generous, *helpful* little sister comes in,' Simon grinned. 'I was hoping you'd agree to drive it over to Turnberry's in the morning to get the new tyre fitted, then bring it back to London for me, Mirry. You could——'

'Simon...no!' their mother broke in, horrified. 'You can't ask *Mirry* to drive that monster of yours, certainly not in London...'

'Oh, Mum! Don't be a spoilsport,' Mirry wailed. So far Simon had only let her take the wheel of his precious Lotus very briefly, and she was dying for the chance to take it for a real run. 'And anyway...' her eyes danced with sly laughter '...I'm going to have nearly two weeks' practice before I need return it.'

'Why, you crafty little...' Aware of his sister's covetous designs on the Lotus, Simon grimaced. 'I guess I walked right into that one. All right, you have my permission to use it while it's in your possession,' he conceded, and then, because his mother still looked worried, added, 'If she drives it straight to Heathrow and leaves it in the staff car park, she won't need to actually drive in London, Mum.'

'But how will she get home again?'

'Mum, I'm not helpless,' Mirry said with exasperated affection. 'I'm quite capable of getting the tube to St Pancras and catching the train home.'

'She needn't even do that, Mum. I'll get someone to phone and let you know the time my flight gets in, then Mirry can meet me at the airport with the car and stay the night with me at the flat. Provided it's not a late arrival, we can have a night out on the town, Mirry.'

She flung herself at him to give him a jubilant hug, her enthusiasm restraining any more maternal objections.

Mirry combined two errands the following morning, dropping Nick off for his speech therapy before taking the Lotus in for its new tyre, then picking Nick up again on her way home. At first she was a little nervous of all that power under the bonnet, but on the return journey her confidence increased, and it took little encouragement from Nick to put her foot down along the dual carriageway.

'Wow! Eighty!' Nick chortled, and with a return to sanity Mirry eased back on the throttle. If she got a speeding ticket her mother would *never* allow her to drive to London. But it was with a feeling of elation that she swished to a halt outside the Dower House, turning to grin at Nick. 'Not a word about me breaking the speed limit,' she warned.

But, in spite of having Simon's car at her disposal and using it at the slightest excuse, Mirry found herself unusually restless that week. Where once Nick had taken up much of her time, he was working in the garden centre most of the day, and though she still participated in the daily work-out in the gym, he was perfectly capable of getting through his exercises unsupervised. Even chauffeuring him to and from his speech therapy sessions was something her mother could easily take over. And, although there were always jobs she could help with around the house, they didn't occupy her mind, and it was something to occupy her mind she was becoming increasingly in need of, if only to stop it dwelling so often on the burgeoning romance between Jay and Annabel.

It was several days before Mirry would admit to herself that the root of her dissatisfaction was the memory of Jay's contempt when, on the first day of their acquaintance, he had asked her what she did to justify her existence besides living off her parents. She had been indignant at the time, but maybe he had been justified in his contempt, she brooded while the comedy programme on the television played on before her unseeing gaze. With few of the advantages Mirry had been blessed with, Jay had nevertheless carved out a successful career for himself, judging by the respect Philip Amis and Alan Charlesworth had for his abilities. Maybe, if Mirry had been able to boast an exciting and fulfilling career, Jay might have had more respect for her.

Mirry straightened in her chair. Wishing wasn't going to get her anywhere. It was high time she did something constructive with her life. The problem was...what? It was only spring now, so even if she was accepted back on to her university course it wouldn't be until the autumn. And somehow the ambition to become an architect had dissipated these last two years, with nothing so far to take its place.

Her glance was drawn to the sofa where her parents sat together, catching them just at the moment when they turned to each other, sharing their laughter as they had shared everything else for the last forty years, and Mirry knew there was something she *did* want—a marriage just like theirs. A man to love who would love her in return, a man to share her life, the bad bits as well as the good. A man to make a home for, to bear his children, rear them in the same love and total security she herself had known.

She had day-dreamed before about the kind of man who could answer all her needs, but this time the usually nebulous dream man had a face, the dream children—two boys and a girl—laughed up at her with Jay's silvery eyes...

Her mother's voice shattered the dream and Mirry blinked to find the programme had finished and both parents looking at her questioningly. 'I'm sorry, did you say something?'

'Where were you, darling? I was beginning to think you'd fallen into a trance.'

Her mother's question was teasing, but for just a moment Mirry felt her illicit thoughts had been blazoned across her face, and even more embarrassingly the colour began to rise in her cheeks.

Cathy Grey managed to restrain her curiosity and repeated the question that had elicited no response before. 'I was only asking if you'd mind doing the supermarket run tomorrow. I need to go to the bank, so I can take Nick for his speech therapy.'

'Sure, I don't mind.' Thursday was the day both the Dower House and the Hall restocked their larders, but as Jay was safely back in London there was no danger of running into him. Mirry squirmed inwardly, wondering how she would be able to look him in the face without remembering the pictures her wayward imagination had just been conjuring up.

'You don't think Martha might enjoy a ride in the Lotus?' Mirry suggested mischievously the following morning as her father handed her the keys to the estate car.

'If you could get her into that thing, I doubt it could accommodate all the shopping,' her mother returned, amusement turning up the corners of her mouth. 'She says she has a list as long as your arm.'

When Martha made exactly the same comment as she climbed into the estate car drawn up at the rear of the Hall, Mirry asked curiously, 'I thought you were all set to retire, Martha. I mean, after Georgie died I got the impression that you didn't fancy working for Jay Elphick.'

'Yes...well...I thought that mother of his'd be queening it here, didn't I?' Martha settled her capacious handbag firmly on her lap as they set off. 'But when he told me she lives in America now... And he did ask ever so nicely if I'd mind staying on a bit, just till he's decided what he's going to do about the house. Well, he won't need me if he does decide to turn it into a hotel, will he?'

'A hotel?' Mirry's foot slipped off the accelerator in shock. Yet shouldn't she have guessed this was coming? Annabel had told her Jay was talking of selling, had even told her his weekend guests were prospective buyers. Even when Keir had mentioned all three men's involvement with Alpha Hotels she had failed to make the connexion. Alpha Hotels, a name synonymous with luxury on a grand scale, all formerly large country houses very similar to Wenlow.

''Course, he's never actually *told* me,' Martha went on. 'But from little bits I happened to overhear...' she shot a sharp glance at Mirry as if daring her to accuse her of eavesdropping '...and with those men going all over the place from the basement to the attics, well, I can put two and two together same as anybody.'

'I'm sure you can, Martha,' Mirry said hollowly. She still felt as if she'd been kicked in the solar plexus, because she had been counting on Jay at least giving her plans serious consideration. 'So how do you feel about the idea, Martha?'

'Me? Can't say as I like it, but then I reckon I'm too old to fret over something I can't change.' The elderly housekeeper let out a gusty sigh. 'Oh, I know as how Sir David was very keen for his son to carry on where he left off, even if the Jayston name had to die out. But, well...it's not everybody's idea of a home, a great house like that. And it's not as if Mr Jay was brought up there, or had any attachment to the place, is it?'

Mirry was forced to agree. Far from having an attachment to Wenlow, Jay had already made it plain he felt only indifference towards the place and downright animosity towards the people, particularly his late father. And it was just possible that her own championing of David and Georgie had only hardened Jay's resolve not to consider their wishes.

'Sorry, Georgie,' she said under her breath, slackening speed as they approached the town of Market Harborough. 'I seem to have done more harm than good.'

'Did you say something?' Martha asked.

'Just that there's no space along here,' Mirry prevaricated, indicating the cars parked nose to the pavement along the edge of the wide High Street.

'Too far back here,' was Martha's opinion, going on at length about her aches and pains while Mirry waited at the traffic lights to turn right into the big car park that had the supermarket on one side and the river Welland on the other.

'Seems to have done very well for himself. Mr Jay, I mean.' They were almost home again, the car weighed down much more heavily than when they had set out, when Martha returned to the subject of the new master of Wenlow. 'Pity his father lost touch with him. He'd have been right proud of what the lad's made of himself, in spite of that mother of his.'

And would presumably do even better for himself out of the sale of Wenlow, Mirry thought. Not that she begrudged him that. David might have wanted his son to take his rightful place in the Wenlow community but, after all, Jay's work and his home, the life he had built for himself, was in London. And, if he was going to disappear back there after the house was sold, maybe that would be best for them all, certainly for herself. So why did the thought make her feel so depressed?

'That's his car!' Martha exclaimed as they turned into the drive, and Mirry's stomach lurched as she too spotted the black Jaguar by the front door. 'Now, how was I to know he was coming back this morning?' Martha fretted as Mirry drove round the rear of the house. 'There's no lunch ready and only that Letty Skirling in the house, dabbing around with a duster.' She was out of the car as soon as it stopped, and through the kitchen door at a trot, leaving Mirry to do the unloading.

Once more she felt that curl of unease as she stepped into the house she had once known as well as her own but where she knew she was no longer welcome. The kitchen was empty, Martha no doubt having gone in search of her boss to explain her absence. With luck,

Mirry decided, she could have all the stuff unloaded and be away before Jay even knew she had crossed his threshold. But even as she hefted the heavy box on to the scrubbed table the baize door opened and Martha came in, still apologising to the man who followed her.

'There's really no hurry, Mrs Barks.' Jay tried to stop the flow. 'I have an appointment in Leicester this afternoon, but not until——' He broke off. 'Mirry!'

'I can soon rustle up a bit of lunch.' Martha pounced on the box. 'Is this the one with the gammon in, Mirry?'

Mirry, who had frozen to the spot like a wild creature scenting danger, saw the frown gathering on Jay's brow. 'Er...no. That's in the one with the meat for the freezer. I'll get it.'

Not even when she was doing his housekeeper a favour was he prepared to hide his dislike, she thought, needled by the injustice. Well, sucks to you, mister! There was a militant sparkle in her dark eyes as she staggered back into the kitchen under another load, a load which was snatched out of her arms so abruptly, she staggered.

'Are there any more?' Jay demanded tersely, the frown still drawing his brows together as he dumped the box on the table for Martha to delve into eagerly.

'Three more,' Mirry challenged before marching out again, only to find Jay dogging her heels. As if seeing her off the premises, she thought, and whirled on him angrily. 'Look, if you object *so* strongly to any of us Greys darkening your doorstep, it's up to you to make alternative arrangements for Martha to do her shopping. As long as you realise there's no way she can get to a supermarket unless *someone* takes her.'

Something flickered in Jay's silvery eyes. It might have been discomfiture, except Mirry thought it unlikely, especially when he went onto suggest, 'Aren't you exaggerating, Mirry?'

She ground her teeth in disbelief when she recalled some of the things he had said about her family, but before she could find her voice he went on, 'Simon didn't complain about his welcome when he came in for coffee before we set off for London.'

'Well, maybe it's just me you object to, then,' Mirry retorted. 'If looks could have killed when you found me in your kitchen...'

'I was annoyed when I saw what you were up to,' he admitted coolly, then took the wind out of her sails when he added, 'Neither you nor Martha should be lifting those loads about. I thought it was one of the advantages of living in the country, having the local tradesmen deliver.'

Mirry was surprised into rueful laughter. 'You *are* behind the times! Local tradesmen are an extinct species, put out of business by the supermarkets, and as we have no buses either, we're dependent on each other out here.'

Jay made no comment. Instead, peering under the tailgate at all the boxes of groceries still in the car, he said, 'I thought there were only three more.'

'There are.' Mirry leaned in to drag them forward. 'The rest are ours and Helen Dutton's.' Picking up the smaller one herself, she set off back to the kitchen.

'About another ten minutes, Mr Jay,' Martha said.

'Fine,' Jay responded, and followed Mirry out to the car again. He lifted out the final box and she closed the tailgate, but as she moved to open the driver's door a hand on her arm detained her. 'As a matter of fact, I'm glad I've seen you.'

She looked up at him, her expression turning to in-credulity when he asked, 'Why didn't you tell me it was you who drew up those conversion plans?'

'I should have thought that was obvious. If you'd had the slightest suspicion *I* had anything to do with it, you'd have turned the idea down out of hand.' She watched the touch of colour run over his cheekbones. 'Anyway, how did you know?'

'I can read,' he derided. 'Your name was at the bottom. So where did you learn to do such a work-manlike job?'

Mirry had forgotten, and cursed herself for the vanity that had prompted her to label her work. 'I'd completed two years as a student of architecture when I came home to help Nick,' she said with a challenging lift of her chin, and had the satisfaction of seeing his eyes widen.

'I see. So are you going to finish your training?'

'I might.' It was pleasant to have disconcerted him, if only in a small way. 'But then again, I might decide to get a job. Because even though I have a small income of my own and *don't* have to live off my parents...' she offered up a prayer of thanks to the young girl she couldn't even remember but whose death and sub-sequent insurance pay-out made it possible for her to refute that accusation '...it would still be another five years before I could begin to earn my living as an architect.'

Her gibe bounced off his thick skin. 'What kind of job?'

Mirry shrugged and slid into the driving seat. 'Maybe converting houses into flats.' She couldn't resist the tongue-in-cheek suggestion.

'You have enough experience to tackle such work?' He looked sceptical.

Well, hadn't she known all along he would doubt her capabilities? With deliberate insouciance she said, 'Nothing to it. Converting Wenlow would be perfectly straightforward, no actual structural alterations. And if I should be faced with a more complex job, then naturally I'd employ a qualified architect,' she finished grandly. Not allowing him time to challenge her, she powered on, 'Anyway, what does it matter to you whether I could do the job or not? You're selling Wenlow, turning it into a hotel.' Seeing that as a good exit line, Mirry reached across to pull the car door closed.

But Jay made no attempt to move, his eyes narrowing. 'Who told you that?' he snapped.

There was no way Mirry was going to get Martha into trouble, even if it meant claiming to be smarter than she was. 'No one told me. Annabel was concerned because you were talking of selling the house, and your weekend guests just happen to run a chain of country house hotels. Just because we live in the country,' she finished with gentle malice, 'doesn't mean we can't add two and two together.'

Jay laughed. Mirry was so astonished, she could only gape at him. 'From what I've seen of you simple country folk, you could run rings round us poor townies any day.' He closed the car door on her firmly, then through the open window added, 'And just for the record, Mirry, nothing's settled yet.'

Mirry didn't know whether to be glad or sorry about this nugget of news, especially later in the day when Andrew seemed even more down than usual. He normally guarded his deepest feelings, so it was a measure of his despair that, at Mirry's sympathetic prompting, he confessed he had phoned Annabel to ask her out that evening, only to be told by Mrs Frost that she rather thought her daughter was seeing Jay.

Mirry offered herself as a substitute, suggesting they spend a few hours at a new roadhouse about five miles away. So it was ironic that they should return home to hear that Jay had spent most of the evening at the Dower House. Andrew and Mirry exchanged glances. So Jay *hadn't* been with Annabel, after all.

'Did he say why he'd come, Mum?' Mirry tried to sound casual.

'No specific reason. Just being neighbourly. Though he was asking about the property market locally,' Cathy added as an afterthought. 'So it looks as if he's giving consideration to your conversion, Mirry.'

That in itself was surprising enough. Even more amazing was that Jay had been at the Dower House at all, seeing that, in his opinion, it was her parents who had broken up his mother's romance with his father. From their placid demeanour he hadn't repeated those accusations. But still Mirry felt uneasy.

The following morning there was a phone call from Abigail Minto, asking if Mirry could come over that afternoon and bring her clarinet. Since an injury to her hand had meant retirement from the concert platform, Abby had begun to climb a new career ladder as a composer, and such a request was not unusual when she was working on something she wanted to try out.

This was an outing where Mirry could safely take Simon's Lotus, and carefully parking it alongside Keir's Mercedes on the gravel sweep she rang the bell. The housekeeper smiled a welcome and told her to go straight through to the sitting-room.

Mirry burst impetuously into the large room at the rear, where the grand piano stood on a dais in the curve of the big window, and stopped dead, her heart seeming to somersault in her breast. Although vaguely aware of several people there, she noticed only one. Their gazes clashed and held, and surely it couldn't be *pleasure* on Jay's face?

Even as she wondered, another voice, heavily accented, broke the thread of tension. 'Mirree...*ma petite*, even more ravishing than ever!' Two arms swept her into an enthusiastic hug, and her surprised mouth was thoroughly kissed.

'Jules!' Mirry exclaimed when he finally released her. 'Abby, you clam, why didn't you tell me?'

'I insist that we give you the surprise.' Jules' arm lingered possessively at her waist.

A quick glance at Jay revealed that he didn't share Keir and Abby's amusement. His face was wooden, his eyes blank, and Mirry knew she had been mistaken that he had seemed pleased to see her.

Though Jules Charpentier played the piano extremely well, it was as a cellist he was building a reputation in the concert halls, and because there was a limited repertoire for the cello he had become a regular visitor at the Minto home, Abigail composing several works especially for him.

Mirry had come to know him well, to know he liked to play the Latin lover to the hilt, to know also it was just a game, so she had never been in danger of taking him seriously. But now, under Jay's blank stare, she found herself playing up to him.

'It's wonderful to see you again, Jules. How long are you staying?' Let Jay see another man could find her attractive, even if he didn't.

'Alas, only until tomorrow, *ma chère*,' Jules mourned, his dark eyes gazing soulfully into hers, until Mirry had to suppress a giggle. 'It is the work. The Festival 'all on Sunday and back to Paris on Monday. But now we make our own music, *n'est-ce pas*?'

'You've finished something new, Abby?'

'For cello, piano and clarinet,' Abby said. 'We're going to record the piano and clarinet parts first, then add the cello to it, so if you're ready...'

'Come on, Jay, we'll leave these artistic types to it,' Keir said. 'We have our own work to do, anyway.' Mirry watched as the two men moved towards the study, Jay never once glancing her way.

But Mirry soon became too absorbed to brood on Jay's antagonism. She and Jules played through the piano and clarinet parts several times under Abby's direction, Mirry stumbling at first but becoming progressively more confident, though she would have preferred one more rehearsal when Abby insisted they could record.

With that on tape, Mirry could sit back and enjoy Jules' superb playing as he added the cello part. They were listening critically for the second time to the final recording of all three instruments, Abby following from the score and making notes where things didn't please her, when Keir and Jay came quietly back into the room. There was a conscious relaxing when the tape had finished, and Mirry was astounded to find it was seven o'clock. The conversation ran on classical music for a while, Jay surprising Mirry with his knowledgeable interest. Yet why should she be surprised? He was obviously a well-educated and cultured man.

He hadn't yet spoken to her directly, so she was unprepared when he suddenly said, 'You seem equally at home with jazz and classical music, Mirry. Have you never thought of taking the clarinet up as a career?'

Having just spent several hours being shown her limitations by two professionals, she laughingly disclaimed, 'Oh, I'll admit to a certain facility, but there's a very wide gap between even a talented amateur and a professional. Besides, I've had no musical education to speak of.'

'The *bouleversé* life of the musician is not for her!' Jules derided the suggestion. 'Mirree is the home-loving girl, yes? Born to be the adored wife of some lucky man and the devoted mother of his children.'

Jay shot him a narrowed glance, as if the other man had surprised him; then, shifting that silvery gaze back to Mirry in a lingering inventory, he drawled, 'You could very well be right, Jules.'

CHAPTER SEVEN

'YOU mean your brother actually trusts you with *this*?'
Jay stopped abruptly beside the low red monster
gleaming in the light from the Mintos' front door.

It was a typical male chauvinist attitude, one that
Mirry was used to and never allowed to bother her. 'As
his only chance of getting it back for weeks is to trust
me to drive it to London for him, he didn't have any
option,' she laughed, opening the driver's door, but Jay
still seemed to doubt the wisdom of taking the passenger
seat.

After Jules' and Jay's embarrassing dissection of her
character, only Mrs Jameson's timely announcement that
dinner was ready spared her blushes. However, the meal
had passed off without further embarrassment, conversation being general and Jay showing a much more relaxed side of his personality. The first time he laughed
aloud at one of her sallies, Mirry was fascinated and
pleased, encouraged to see if she could prompt a repeat
of this phenomenon and elated each time she succeeded.

By the time they returned to the sitting-room, Mirry's
sparkle had affected them all. A musical argument, and
Mirry's assertion that everything was grist to the jazz
musician's mill, had her demonstrating a jazzed-up
version of one of the themes from Mozart's *Eine Kleine
Nachtmusik*, to Jules' cries of 'Sacrilege!'

Keir joined her on the piano and they romped through
several jazz classics until Jules could stand it no longer

and brought his cello into a spirited rendition of 'The Dark Town Strutter's Ball', until a stifled yawn from Abby, whose pregnancy was only about eight weeks off full term, had Mirry putting her clarinet away and declaring it was high time she went home. It had been Jay himself who'd suggested she could give him a lift, as he didn't have his car there.

With a rueful, 'I hope I don't live to regret this,' Jay folded himself into the low-slung Lotus, and, stifling her laughter, Mirry slid in beside him, clipping on the seatbelt. Flipping a final wave at the three people standing in the doorway, and missing Jules' parting riposte as the ignition fired with a throaty roar, she reversed neatly round Keir's Mercedes and moved forward along the drive, pausing between the gateposts with their pineapple finials and turning into the winding, undulating lane that would take them back to Wenlow.

'I suppose you know that Frenchman fancies you,' Jay commented.

Mirry gurgled with laughter as the car gathered speed, the powerful headlights slashing through the darkness. 'You mean that Charles Boyer performance of his? Nonsense, he treats every female like that. He can't help it.'

The whole evening had turned out so much better than she had feared; Jay had been so much more approachable and he was sitting beside her now, only a handspan away, the woody scent of his aftershave drifting towards her now and again, and something more, an indefinable *male* scent she had never noticed with her brothers. She felt sparklingly alive and quite ridiculously happy.

'You seemed so delighted to see him, I thought he must be the man in your life.'

So Jay had noticed not all men treated her as if she had a bad case of plague. 'Of course I was delighted to see him. Jules is great fun. What girl wouldn't enjoy having a famous musician flirting with her and kissing her hand?' She changed gear as she approached the narrow, hump-backed bridge over the canal. 'Hold tight!'

Jay groaned as he left his stomach behind, but Mirry was busy smoothly negotiating the right-angled bend immediately beyond. 'I must say you can handle this thing,' he allowed grudgingly.

'Why, thank you, kind sir.' Mirry flashed him a cheeky grin. 'As a matter of fact I'm really looking forward to getting it on the motorway next week.'

'You were serious, then? About taking it to London?' The car lifted slightly as they passed the much lower bridge over the stream that fed the lake at Wenlow.

'Well, Heathrow,' Mirry conceded. 'Simon'll drive us both into London from there. We're going to have a night on the town before I catch the train home.'

'When, next week?' Jay asked, grabbing the dashboard to steady himself as the car snaked into a right-hand turn at the deserted crossroads.

'Wednesday.' Mirry put on a spurt along a comparatively straight stretch before braking smoothly for the bend and continuing to brake as she approached the Wenlow drive.

Out of pure mischief she asked, 'Do you want me to drop you at the gate, or am I to be allowed on Wenlow property long enough to take you to your door?'

Jay made an explosive sound of annoyance, and for a moment Mirry was afraid she'd gone too far with her teasing. Then he said tightly, 'You'll take me to the door, of course, and then you'll come into the house for a drink. I need to talk to you.'

Mirry obediently swept past the little church and into the drive, speculating what he could want with her.

Jay was out of the car before she had doused the lights and released her seat-belt, coming round to help her out. Her skin seemed to tingle under his touch, an entirely pleasurable sensation, and she made no move to pull away as he kept his hand beneath her elbow to escort her indoors.

Jay made straight for the library. Nothing had changed since her last traumatic visit to the room when she'd been caught red-handed searching the desk, except now there was a computer squatting on top of it.

'I need to keep in touch with things while I'm here,' Jay explained as he saw her looking at it. 'But that particular model's not ideal. That's what I was consulting Keir about today. He's going to fix me up with one better suited to my needs. What can I get you to drink?'

Because she was driving, Mirry had limited herself to one small glass of wine with her dinner, and felt she could indulge herself a little now, asking for a small brandy with a lot of ginger ale. 'Nick's the one who's into computers,' she said, examining the set-up on the desk with interest. 'Or rather, he was...'

Jay brought her drink across. 'You mean he lost interest, or the ability to understand?'

She shrugged sadly. 'I wish I knew! We had to start from scratch with him, you know: teach him to sit up, to stand, to feed and wash himself and eventually to walk and talk.'

It had been gruelling work, exercising Nick's helpless body. For every waking minute he'd needed to be pummelled and stimulated. Disheartening work too, when each improvement had been so slow in coming and sometimes so infinitesimal that Mirry, impatient for miracles, had often cried tears of frustration into her pillow at night. But each small improvement had added up, so that by the end of a year Nick had been able to stand, supported by a metal walker, and even to shuffle a few steps. And the gymnasium they had fitted out in the old dairy had continued the improvement, as speech therapy was still improving his articulation.

'As time went on he seemed to have more and more recall of things he knew before the accident, and of course we re-introduced him to his computer,' she went on, 'taught him to play some of the games because it helped his co-ordination. But he's never attempted to do anything else with it, even though I've tried to prompt him.'

Jay stared down at the glass in his hand. 'I'd no idea things had been so bad for him,' he muttered. 'That's one of the things I wanted to talk to you about, to apologise for that cheap crack of mine about you living off your parents. It was indefensible when I knew nothing about you or your circumstances.'

Mirry had no idea what had changed his opinion, but there was no stopping the pleased smile that lit her small face. 'Apology accepted,' she said promptly, then with an infectious smile added, 'Don't look so worried, Jay. With five brothers, I'm not such a tender little plant that an unkind word can throw me into a decline.'

A reluctant smile hovered round the mouth that had been a lot less buttoned up tonight. 'I can well imagine! All the same, if I'd known you'd given up your career in order to help your brother, I'd never have made that unfortunate remark.'

Now he was embarrassing her. 'Please... don't make me out to be some kind of Pollyanna. I can assure you my motives were very selfish. If there *was* going to be a way back to normality for Nick, I meant to be part of it. In any case, it was Eleanor—William's wife—who was responsible for his recovery. I only carried out her instructions.'

'Look, won't you sit down?' Belatedly remembering his manners, Jay indicated the leather sofa in front of the empty fireplace. 'Are you cold?'

Mirry sank down on to the sofa, shaking her head, but Jay switched on the electric fire anyway before sitting down himself. 'As this seems to be my night for eating humble pie,' he said, 'I have to tell you I went to see Mr Golding yesterday.'

'The solicitor?' Mirry's eyes were round and questioning as she wondered what was coming next.

Jay took a fortifying swallow of his drink and contemplated the heavy cut-glass tumbler. 'It wasn't only what you said—about checking with him where my mother's income had come from...' Mirry's heart began to beat in slow, heavy thuds as she watched the frown gathering on his face. 'There were a number of things that didn't add up. The disconcerting friendliness of all you Greys, for a start, though one of them...' that fugitive smile lurked around his beautiful mouth again '...had the sting of a scorpion when she was provoked.'

Mirry gave a gasping laugh which she quickly stifled, reluctant to interrupt him.

'I was puzzled why *I* should be the main beneficiary in Lady Jayston's will when she had plenty of relatives of her own. It didn't match the picture I'd always had of her, and neither for that matter did the way people talked about her here. But the real facer was learning she'd been confined to a wheelchair all those years, even while my mother——'

He lifted his glass to his lips again, found it was empty and got up to refill it, offering replenishment to Mirry, who refused. 'So yesterday I went to see Mr Golding, and found what you'd claimed was true. Everything... our home, the food we ate, the clothes we wore, my school fees and the allowance that saw me through university, even the money I came into on my twenty-first birthday, were all provided by the man I'd always believed had betrayed my mother and turned his back on me.'

'Oh, Jay... I'm so sorry.' Mirry's hand reached out to clasp his compassionately.

He looked down at it. 'Sorry?' Although his words had been emotive, his expression had been devoid of any feeling, except now, a mild surprise. 'Why should you be sorry when you've been proved right?'

'Because it must have come as a shock to you,' she said, her teeth worrying her lower lip. She ought to be pleased that Jay now knew the truth, but instead she was assailed by sudden doubts. 'Because I've only just re-alised that being right doesn't justify hurting someone, destroying their illusions.'

'Illusions?' Jay stared at her in blank incomprehension. 'I've never been aware I *had* any illusions.'

It was difficult, not knowing how close Jay and his mother were, but Valerie *had* brought him up, had been the only family he had known, and Mirry didn't want to be responsible for damaging that relationship.

'I—I'm sure your mother must have had reasons for—for not being entirely truthful with you, Jay,' she said, choosing her words carefully. 'I mean, I *can* understand why she couldn't let you go when you were a baby, and even why she wouldn't ever want you to know she had refused to allow David and Georgie to adopt you. She must have been afraid you'd resent her for it.'

'So you think you can see into my mother's mind now, do you?' His sardonic jeer shattered their brief rapport.

Mirry flushed. 'No, of course I don't, but I'm a woman and I know in her position *I* wouldn't have been able to give up my baby either, in spite of the difficulties of being a single mother.'

Something flickered in those silvery-grey eyes and then was gone, his face completely expressionless as he asked, 'And in my mother's place would you have handed the child you couldn't bear to part with over to a series of unsupervised au pair girls? Would you have packed him off to boarding-school before he was eight years old and made it obvious he was a damned nuisance when he had to be at home for the school holidays?'

He spoke dispassionately, but Mirry was appalled at the picture he painted. 'That—that happened to you?' she whispered. 'Oh, Jay, if only your father had known...'

'You think he would have cared?'

His tone was so disbelieving that she said fiercely, 'Yes! Yes, of course, he would. He'd have moved heaven and earth——'

'Since it wouldn't have taken anything like that much effort to find out how my mother was spending his money,' Jay dismissed, 'you must forgive me if I'm not convinced.'

Mirry opened her mouth to argue the point, then closed it again. Maybe David *should* have asserted himself more over his son's upbringing. She sighed, remembering her mother telling her it had been David who had been the vulnerable one in that affair. She said slowly, 'Your father was a very innocent man in many ways. I don't think it would have occurred to him that your mother wasn't giving you all the loving care you needed, not when she had always refused to give you up.'

Jay merely shrugged, as if bored with the conversation. 'Oh, well, it hardly matters now.'

'Of course it matters——' Mirry began distressfully, when the door opened with a rush and an eager voice said,

'I got back earlier than I expected, Jay, and when I saw the lights on and the car outside...'

Annabel came right into the room, closing the door behind her, glancing quickly at Mirry then back to Jay, her expression one of expectant curiosity. 'Hello, Mirry. I hope I'm not interrupting...'

Mirry watched, hiding her frustration, as Jay sprang to his feet with pleased relief. 'We were just having a drink. Come and join us, Annabel.' He urged her into his own place on the sofa and crossed to the drinks tray. 'What will you have?'

'Oh, my usual, please, Jay. That's if you're sure I'm not in the way? When I recognised the car outside I thought you must be discussing the conversion plans.

Does that mean you've finally decided to go ahead with it?'

Some of the warmth faded from Jay's face as he said repressively, 'I've not thought any more about that, let alone had reason to discuss it.'

'Oh.' Annabel's disappointment was apparent, and in the sidelong glance she flicked at Mirry was the unspoken question: well, what *have* you been talking about, then? And maybe her piqued curiosity was justified, Mirry thought with a hollow feeling in the pit of her stomach. If Annabel felt able to walk into the house unannounced and be sure of the kind of welcome she had met with from Jay, then their relationship must be deepening rapidly.

'I gave Jay a lift home from the Mintos', that's all,' she explained hurriedly, pushing herself up from the low couch. 'And you're not interrupting at all, Annabel. It's time I was leaving.'

Annabel looked pleased, and, expecting to see the same feeling reflected in Jay's expression as he took her glass, she was surprised to see his mouth drawn into a tight line. 'You don't have to rush off, Mirry,' he protested.

The thought of playing gooseberry, even for a few minutes, was more than she could stomach. 'I've still got to get Simon's pride and joy home safely. No, don't bother to see me out, Jay. I'm sure you and Annabel have plenty to talk about. Goodnight.' She hurried to the door without looking at either of them again, almost running as she crossed the big hall, the gravel spurting from beneath the Lotus's wheels as she accelerated away. Because another thought had just occurred to her; if Annabel was sure enough of her welcome to walk into

Jay's home unannounced *at this time of night*, were they already lovers?

As she had anticipated, Mirry thoroughly enjoyed driving the Lotus back to London, though she did have a few hairy moments, feeling horribly close to the ground and vulnerable compared to the juggernaut lorries. But she had timed it well and only had half an hour to hang about at the airport before she saw Simon, even more handsome in his uniform, hurrying towards her.

'You made it in one piece, then?' The relief on his face was evidence that he'd felt some concern, but, grinning at him, Mirry pretended those qualms had been only for his car.

'As you see, and not a dent, not a scratch, not even a fingerprint. Was it a good flight?'

'Hot and uneventful.' Even so, on the drive into London he kept her entertained with some of his repeatable experiences.

Simon's flat was in Fulham, and at that time in the afternoon he was able to find a parking space quite close. Taking his flight bag and Mirry's overnight bag out of the boot, he shepherded her into the lift and up to the fifth floor. The stale air of rooms shut up for several weeks met them as he pushed open the front door. Mirry wrinkled her nose, and while Simon bent to pick up the mail that had accumulated in his absence she crossed to the sitting-room window and flung it open.

Looking around she said, 'This place doesn't look any more like a home than it did when you moved in five years ago.'

Simon looked up from sorting through his letters. 'Why? What's the matter with it?'

'It's so—so bare! Why don't you have more personal things about? A few pictures on the walls, some ornaments and plants. Even a couple of bright cushions on the sofa.'

'You could be right about the cushions,' he conceded, 'but spare me the knick-knacks. Anyway, I never spend enough time here to look on it as home.'

And Mirry was aware that when he *was* here, it wasn't always alone, having often had her phone calls to him answered by a variety of female voices. Thinking of her two eldest brothers happily married, and of Andrew, who would like to be if only Annabel felt the same way, she asked curiously, 'Haven't you ever felt the urge to settle down with one woman, Simon? To make a real home?'

He grimaced, then surprised her by saying, 'Chance'd be a fine thing! If I found the right girl, how does a gypsy like me compete with the home-based chaps?'

His attention returned to his mail. 'Hand-delivered! P'raps some little chick's waiting with bated breath for my return…' He tore the letter open, scanning the single sheet quickly. 'Well, what do you know! You did bring something fancy to wear tonight, Mirry?'

'Yes, but—— Look, if that's in invitation from a girl-friend, you don't have to worry about me. I can——'

'Nothing like that. It's from Jay Elphick.'

'Jay?' Mirry was incredulous. She hadn't seen him since she'd given him the lift home in the Lotus, though she knew from a very disgruntled Annabel that he had returned to London. The last thing she had expected was to have any contact with him on this visit. 'Wh—what does he want?'

'Our company for the evening, apparently.' Simon was already punching numbers into the phone. 'Jay? Simon

Grey. Just got back and found your note. Sure she is.'
He looked across at Mirry, grinning as he listened. 'Like
that, is it? Yes, we'll enjoy that. Oh, and as to your
other suggestion, I'll accept with thanks on Mirry's
behalf.' Mirry was almost exploding with indignant
curiosity while he listened again, his grin broadening.
'That gives us an hour and a half. Should be long
enough, even for Mirry. Right, Jay, see you then.'

'And just what was all that about, brother dear?'
Mirry demanded with a militant sparkle in her eyes.

'That's a question I hoped you'd be able to answer.'
Simon surveyed her, one eyebrow rising speculatively.
'What have you been doing to the poor man that he
needs me as a go-between?'

To her annoyance, Mirry felt the colour rising in her
cheeks. 'I haven't the faintest idea what you're talking
about.'

Simon's brows rose even higher. 'No idea why he
should think the only way he'll get to see you is to have
me along as well?'

'He didn't tell you that? He couldn't have!' she protested, her eyes widening. 'Either you misunderstood or
you're deliberately teasing, Simon. Jay disliked me on
sight.'

Simon shook his head pityingly. 'If there's a mis-
understanding, I don't think it's on *my* part.' Picking
up her bag, he carried it into the guest-room. 'I suppose
I'll have to give you first crack at the bathroom, but
don't hog it.'

Mirry puzzled over this surprising development as she
showered. Not that she could take Simon's teasing
seriously. There was a lot her brother didn't know: Jay's
antagonism towards the Greys and the reasons behind

it, for one thing, his romantic involvement with Annabel
for another. But surely this invitation had to be in the
nature of an olive branch? It must mean that the things
Jay had learned since his arrival at Wenlow had softened
his attitude.

Banging on Simon's door to let him know the
bathroom was free, Mirry went back to her own room,
wondering as she studied herself in the mirror how even
someone as partial as a brother could imagine Jay might
find her attractive. She supposed 'elfin' was the best that
could be said for her looks, with her pointed chin and
tip-tilted nose. At least the curl in her hair was natural,
and she did have splendid teeth, she told her derisive
reflection. It was probably a little more eyeshadow and
mascara than usual that brought out the sparkle in her
brown eyes, and her too wide mouth *would* keep turning
up at the corners as she tried to gloss it with a peachy
lipstick, for, although she was trying to use her common
sense, a sparkly excitement was like champagne in her
veins.

The clothes she had brought with her for the evening
had been chosen for their uncrushable qualities: an ankle-
length black wrap-round skirt in an embossed silky material, finely pleated, and a silky cream blouson top with
an elasticated waistband and scooped-out neckline, but
it was an outfit that always made her feel good, the skirt
rippling sensuously around her as she moved, giving an
occasional glimpse of slender leg, the blouse softly feminine. Very feminine too, were the fragile black sandals
with their high, spindly heels that she slipped on her
narrow feet, and the touches of Ivoire on her pulse spots.

Simon was lounging on the sofa in the sitting-room
when she finally emerged. He looked her over with

brotherly appraisal. 'Hmm. I'm beginning to see why Jay's smitten.'

'Oh, you...' Mirry derided, but her expression was unconsciously wistful. 'You ought to write novels, with your imagination.' She was beginning to realise how embarrassing this evening could be if she didn't rid Simon of his misapprehension. What the devil *had* Jay said to him to start him on this tack, anyway? 'If Jay's smitten with anyone, then it's Annabel. I was there when they met. He took one look at her and I ceased to exist.'

'You don't fancy him yourself?' Simon looked quizzical.

Her brother was too astute to let her get away with a flat denial, so she said lightly, 'I quite fancy Richard Gere too, but I know my limitations. I'll be happy to settle for Jay as a cousin.'

She must have been convincing, because Simon shrugged. 'Maybe it's just as well. I can't see Mum and Dad taking to the idea of Valerie Elphick as your mother-in-law.'

That came a little too close to her secret dream for comfort, but the idea of it being Jay's dream too was laughable.

The doorbell brought the discussion to a close. Mirry took a deep breath to try to slow the sudden acceleration of her heartbeat as she listened to Simon's cheerful, 'Come in, Jay. Time for a drink?'

The two men came in together. Both were immaculate in dinner-jacket and black tie, and, though there was no doubting that Simon was the better-looking, it was to Jay that her eyes were inexorably drawn, her tongue sneaking out to moisten suddenly dry lips.

'A drink?' Jay said vaguely, his silvery gaze sweeping Mirry from head to toe. 'Oh, no thanks, Simon, I'm driving.'

'Well, we're both ready.' Simon picked up Mirry's shawl, galvanising her into action.

'This is very handsome of you, Jay.' She sent him a beaming smile, determined to quell the turbulent feelings he aroused in her and just enjoy this unexpected evening.

He merely inclined his head, watching her silently as she walked past him and through the door. They were in the lift when he said, 'You got the car to London in one piece, then?' and Mirry began to tell him about her journey, hamming up her story to make him laugh, knowing she was prattling but unable to stop until, walking out of the building, the sight of an attractive, dark-haired woman getting out of the passenger seat of Jay's car dried up the flow.

'Sorry to keep you waiting, Kate,' Jay was saying. 'Let me introduce you to Mirry Grey and her brother Simon.'

The woman smiled up at him with the familiarity of long acquaintance. 'I was just about to congratulate you for being so quick.' She transferred her smile to Mirry and Simon, holding out her hand. 'Hello, I'm Kate Redding.'

As she shook hands, Mirry found herself thinking, so this is the kind of woman who shares his life in London. Less sophisticated than she had expected, but definitely not less beautiful with her shining cap of expertly cut dark hair and a dress that was surely couture beneath the short mink jacket. She wondered if Annabel knew of Kate's existence, then she told herself it was none of her business as she slid into the rear seat with Simon beside her.

As Jay drove them into the West End, Kate entertained them with the story of a flat in Fulham she had once shared with three other girls. She was nice, Mirry decided, liking her natural warmth, though maybe Simon was showing a little too plainly how much he liked her, too.

When they left the car parked in a side street, she would have taken her brother's arm, but somehow Jay was there instead. 'You're looking very beautiful tonight, Mirry,' he said, one hand lightly at her waist as he piloted her along the pavement.

'Th-thank you.' Astonished at his compliment, she gazed up at him.

But there was no mockery or sarcasm in the silvery eyes that returned her gaze, only a wry twist of his mouth as he said, 'Why so surprised? Did you think I hadn't noticed?'

'I—er—no——' It was a new experience for Mirry to find herself tongue-tied, and involuntarily she glanced back over her shoulder, but Kate was busily chattering to Simon and appeared not to notice.

'Kate works for Wren Interiors,' Jay said, as if that would explain everything. 'They do all the interior designs for Alpha Hotels. I thought you'd like to meet her.'

Mirry found her widening gaze trapped once again by his, but he added nothing more, leaving her to wonder at his motive. Was he still intending to turn Wenlow into a hotel, then? Or had he remembered her rash statement about going into interior design herself? Was this introduction an attempt to help her get a job? But surely he must realise a firm like Kate's would never look at someone as inexperienced as herself?

With all these thoughts whirling inside her head, she hardly noticed where they were going until Jay held the door open for her to step inside the discreetly luxurious restaurant.

The *maître d'* stepped forward with a formal smile of welcome and murmured, 'Good evening, Mr Elphick.' Then his smile warmed to one of real pleasure. 'And Miss Grey! How delightful. Your brother is still improving, I trust?'

'Yes, indeed, thank you, Charles,' Mirry responded, returning his smile with interest; she was conscious of Jay's surprise, but before he could make any comment Charles was ushering them through to the bar and clicking his fingers for a waiter.

'I wish I could dine at a place like this often enough for the staff to recognise me,' Kate laughed, as they settled themselves round a small table.

'I'd have thought a pretty girl like you would rarely have an evening at home,' Simon said gallantly, taking a menu from Charles with a word of thanks.

Kate's face lit with pleasure. 'You don't know what that's done for my self-esteem, Simon, both the "pretty" and the "girl", though I'm obliged to point out I left my girlhood behind some time ago. Maybe I could go out more often if I chose, but naturally I like to spend the time when I'm not working with my little girls.'

Simon's gaze dropped to the rings on her left hand. 'You're married.' His voice was curiously flat.

'I'm a widow,' Kate said quietly. 'I thought Jay would have told you.'

'I'm sorry.' Simon's hand reached out to cover hers.

'Oh, don't let me put a damper on the evening. It's been nearly three years, after all. Jay winkles me out of my domesticity from time to time.' She smiled at him across the table. 'He was Steven's oldest friend, and is also godfather to the twins.'

That put rather a different light on Jay's relationship with Kate, and Mirry couldn't deny a lightening of her spirits. 'Twins, Kate? How lovely! You must hate having to leave them to go to work.'

Kate nodded. 'Yes, I do, but please...I promised myself I wouldn't even mention my kids tonight.'

'Why ever not?' Simon asked. 'I'd have thought they'd be your favourite topic of conversation.'

'Mine, yes, but not other people's,' Kate laughed.

'Oh, I don't know,' Simon reflected. 'I've always fancied the idea of having daughters myself.'

'Simon comes from a big family, Kate,' Jay put in. 'Not only Mirry, but four brothers too.'

'*And* any number of foster brothers and sisters,' Simon added. 'Our house was always swarming with kids.'

'Really?' Kate looked intrigued. 'Your parents must be very remarkable people.'

'We think so, don't we, Mirry?' Simon threw an affectionate arm around his sister's shoulders.

'Oh, yes,' Mirry agreed, an unconscious challenge in the tilt of her chin as she looked at Jay. 'They're something special.'

To her surprise he said softly, 'I'd already begun to work that out for myself.'

He held Mirry's astonished gaze. Was he trying to tell her he no longer bore a grudge, that his invitation tonight was a genuine attempt to make a new start? Suddenly she felt so happy, her small faced was bathed in its radiance, giving her a sparkling beauty she was unaware of herself, but which made the man staring at her swallow hard.

A waiter brought their drinks, while another took their orders for dinner. When they'd all chosen, Kate began to ask Simon about the foster brothers and sisters who had shared his home, but Jay made no attempt to join in, drawing his chair closer to Mirry and commenting wryly, 'Here I was, thinking I'd be introducing you to one of the fleshpots of London, only to find you know it better than I do.'

She laughed. 'Wenlow isn't Outer Mongolia, you know, and Simon's flat gives us all a base in London. Actually, I spent quite a lot of time with him when I was at university. Canterbury's a long way from Wenlow for a weekend, and during some of my vacations I was lucky enough to be taken on for work experience by Haslam Tenniel.' She watched his brows rise at the name of one of London's leading architects. 'Not that I dined at places like this often,' she added, her dark eyes dancing, 'but this was always my favourite for a special celebration.'

'Then either it was a stroke of genius on my part choosing it tonight, or I'm more attuned to your tastes than I'd dared hope,' Jay murmured, the hard lines of his face softening into a teasing smile.

Mirry stared at him, her lips parted on a startled breath. Was Jay *flirting* with her? Before she could be sure, a booming voice rang out, 'Mirry! Mirry Grey!'

She leapt to her feet with a crow of pure delight as she saw the thick-set man with a mane of pure white hair powering across the room towards her. 'Uncle John! Or should I show more respect and call you Lord Shilbury now?' she asked mischievously, knowing the industri-

alist had been given a life peerage in the New Year's
Honours list.

'Cheeky minx.' He landed a smacking kiss on her
cheek. 'And what do you mean by coming to London
without letting me know?'

'I'm only staying overnight,' she said regretfully.

'Lydia'll be furious she's missed you. She's in Paris
till the weekend. Simon, you old son of a gun!'

While he shook her brother's hand, Mirry realised this
meeting couldn't have been more opportune. It was an
ideal chance to draw Jay into his father's circle of friends.

'Uncle John, let me introduce you. Kate
Redding...Lord Shilbury.' She paused while a goggle-
eyed Kate took the proffered hand and murmured something polite; then, keeping her eyes demurely lowered to
hide her glee, she continued, '...and this is Jay Elphick.'

'Mr Elphick.' About to take Jay's hand, John Shilbury
did a double-take. 'Did you say *Jay Elphick*? David's
boy?'

Unable to hide her laughter at the surprise she had
sprung on him, Mirry nodded. 'None other.'

John pumped the stunned Jay's hand enthusiastically.
'David's boy! Well, damn me! I'm delighted to meet you
at long last. Delighted.'

Jay's 'Thank you, sir,' was strangled, but Lord
Shilbury, the bit between his teeth, seemed not to notice.

'Should have happened years ago. Always thought
your father was wrong-headed to let your mother call
the shots, but that's what guilt can do to a man. Too
late to change things now, and David's made sure you're
where you belong at last.' He became aware of a man
who had come up to hover at his elbow. 'Dammit, I
have to go, my guests have arrived. Look, we must get

together some time, Jay. Your father honoured me with his friendship and I hope you'll do the same.'

There was an odd little silence when he moved away. Kate broke it with a breathless, 'Lord Shilbury's your *uncle*?'

Simon hooted. 'We've known him all our lives, but Mirry's the only one with the cheek to call him uncle. The rest of us are much more respectful.'

'Don't listen to him,' Mirry advised. 'John Shilbury's just a teddy bear.'

'I rather doubt his business opponents see him in that light,' Jay said drily. 'Ah, I think our table's ready.'

Kate was obviously bursting with curiosity but too polite to ask questions, and though the conversation over dinner was lively, several times Mirry caught Jay staring across the restaurant to where the industrialist was entertaining his guests. She couldn't define his expression, but something seemed to have shaken him.

Was he surprised that his father, whose livelihood and interests were wholly centred on country pursuits, had been on such terms of friendship with a hard-headed business tycoon like John Shilbury? Well, it *was* an unlikely friendship, yet it had lasted since university days, but then both David and Georgie had had a gift for making—and keeping—friends.

What a difference it would have made to Jay's life had his mother allowed the adoption! Georgie would never have left his upbringing to au pair girls, neither would David have shuffled him off to school so young. He would have grown up knowing the security of two loving parents, the affection of a large extended family. He, too, would have been calling John Shilbury 'uncle'.

And Mirry felt an overpowering yearning to make up for all Jay had missed, to fill his life with love and such happiness that he would forget the years of loneliness and alienation.

CHAPTER EIGHT

It was nearly lunch time before Simon emerged from his room the next morning. 'How do you always manage to look so bright-eyed and bushy-tailed?' he complained, yawning.

'A life of unsullied purity,' Mirry quipped, glad that her restless night didn't show, or Simon would have tried to make something of it.

They had gone on to a club after leaving the restaurant, Jay becoming flatteringly attentive, much to the upset of Mirry's equilibrium, especially when they danced. Even now, in the cold light of morning, she still seemed to feel the imprint of his body against hers as they moved to the music. Although she had never had a serious romance, she had danced with plenty of men, but never had she seemed to *fit* with a partner before, as if their bodies were made to complement each other. The brush of his thighs against hers had made her feel as if her bones were melting.

And yet she had known it was dangerous to give in to these feelings when she was only too aware that Jay didn't return them. To take her mind off the delicious sensations his nearness had been arousing, she'd said brightly, 'Kate and Simon seem to be getting on well, don't they? I like Kate.'

'Good.' He'd drawn her a little closer as he avoided another couple.

113

Mirry had drawn in a trembling breath, her heart beating so hard she was afraid he would be aware of it. 'D-don't you mind?' she'd persisted. 'That Kate and Simon seem attracted, I mean?'

'No, I don't mind,' he'd said against her hair, his breath moving the curling tendrils.

She'd stared fixedly over his shoulder, fighting the temptation to melt against him. 'I always thought Simon was the love 'em and leave 'em type,' she'd babbled on, using words as a shield. 'But something he said tonight makes me think he'd love to settle down, given the right woman.'

'Mirry...' She had been forced to look up at him, and discovered those frosty silver eyes could soften with warm amusement. Her mouth had gone dry. 'Shut up, huh?' He'd gathered her close and Mirry had given up. Just this once, just for tonight she would allow herself to dream.

Mirry abandoned the salad she was preparing for lunch to pour her brother a mug of coffee, asking, 'How long before you're off again?'

'Three days.' He sat down at the breakfast bar, watching his sister as she resumed the lunch preparations. 'I could get used to being looked after,' he grinned. And then, as if the two statements were connected, 'I'm seeing Kate again tomorrow. It's all right,' he added quickly. 'I asked if I was stepping on Jay's toes and she said definitely not.'

Mirry wondered if Simon had found what he was looking for in the young widow, a woman mature and stable enough not to turn to other men when he had to be away. 'I liked her,' she said encouragingly.

But Simon didn't rise to her prompting. 'What time's Jay collecting you?' he asked.

She had found an empty honey jar to mix the French dressing in, and hoped the vigorous shaking would account for her suddenly reddened cheeks. 'Two-thirty. And you might have told me about his offer, Simon.'

When Jay had driven them back to the flat last night he had walked Mirry into the building while Simon was saying his farewells to Kate. 'You don't have to get off first thing in the morning, do you?' he asked.

For a moment she looked at him blankly. 'Oh, my train, you mean.'

'Train? Don't be silly. Your brother told me you'd accepted my offer of a lift. Only it would help me if you could make it early afternoon.'

The prospect of spending more time in his company was blissful. 'You're going home tomorrow? Oh, thank you, a lift would be splendid. And whatever time suits you, of course.' She was trying not to sound too eager, unaware that her feelings were emblazoned across her expressive face.

'Thank *you*. I can't remember when I've enjoyed an evening more.' His eyes were on her tremulously smiling mouth, and as he moved his head towards her Mirry swayed to meet him, as if drawn by a magnet. His mouth brushed hers softly, sweetly, parting her lips so seductively that all memory of that first, punishing kiss was blotted out. The softness of his mouth firmed to a demand she responded to helplessly. Her heart fluttered like a trapped bird, and as her eyelids closed the delicious sensations intensified: the slight abrasiveness of his chin, the crispness of his hair at the nape of his neck, the intoxicating male scent of him.

When he finally drew away, her eyelids fluttered up and she looked at him dazedly, only then realising that somehow, during that devastating kiss, her hands had crept round his neck. Colour flared in her cheeks as she let her arms fall to her sides.

'For a pint-size, you certainly pack a punch,' Jay said, and her cheeks burned hotter, her lashes lowering to hide her confusion. 'Two-thirty tomorrow suit you?' he asked, and she nodded. He kissed her again, swiftly and firmly. 'Goodnight then, Mirry. Sleep tight.'

Of course, she'd hardly slept at all, and now her body seemed poised in anticipation of seeing him again.

Which made it such a crashing disappointment when, promptly at two-thirty, she found a stranger on the doorstep. He explained that Mr Elphick had been unavoidably delayed and he had been instructed to collect her instead.

'Traffic's not too bad today. It shouldn't take us long,' the chauffeur commented as the car moved off. But Mirry was too disappointed to care, or to take any interest in their route, so she was startled when, after only about twenty minutes, the car suddenly turned, swooping down into an underground car park.

The man got out and opened her door, and because he obviously expected it, she got out too, for the first time feeling alarm, until he said, 'Mr Elphick should be through by now. If you'd like to come this way, miss.'

She followed him to a lift and the next moment was shooting upwards, watching the figures flash, three...six...nine. The lift stopped and the doors opened. They were in a plushly carpeted foyer where a glossy blonde receptionist sat on guard. 'Miss Grey for Mr

Elphick,' the chauffeur said, and Mirry found herself being examined by astonished blue eyes.

'If you'll come this way, Miss Grey...' The girl led her along a corridor, tapped on a door half-way down and pushed it open. 'Miss Grey's here, Carol.'

This room too was carpeted, but much more work-manlike, with a large desk guarding a communicating door and another in the corner where a girl was typing rapidly. The woman at the larger desk stood up, a woman in her forties, Mirry judged, very smart and efficient-looking but with a friendly smile. She just had time for the fleeting thought that Jay must hold an important position to warrant *two* secretaries when the elder one said, 'Hello, Miss Grey. I'm Carol Thorpe.'

As they shook hands she went on, 'I'm sorry about the delay, but it shouldn't be long now.' She leaned across the desk to press down the intercom. 'Miss Grey has arrived, Mr Elphick.' Back came Jay's disembodied voice, 'Thank you, Carol, we're almost through.'

By now Mirry was feeling euphoric because she would be travelling home with Jay, after all, but before she could say she didn't mind waiting, the phone was claiming the secretary's attention. While she waited it seemed to ring again every time the receiver was replaced, and each time Carol told the caller Mr Elphick was not there and proceeded to deal with the matter herself.

Mirry was so fascinated, she jumped when the inner door suddenly opened, a disgruntled male voice issuing ahead of the speaker. 'I was told you had a liking for a gamble, and nerve enough to turn a risk into a profit.'

'But I only gamble on certainties.' Jay's response was silkily smooth to cover the underlying steel as he followed the other man through the door. His eyes flicked to Mirry, but he gave no sign of recognition as he went on, 'The only certainty with your proposition is that *you* will make a profit. Good day, Mr Fenton.'

Not until the unfortunate Mr Fenton had beaten a retreat did Jay turn to Mirry. Dressed as he had been when she had first met him, in a grey business suit with a white shirt and subdued tie, his hair brushed smooth, his shoes with a polish you could see your face in, he was every inch the successful businessman, at home in his own world, his authority sitting on him as naturally as a second skin. With a flash of insight, Mirry guessed that this was where he was most comfortable because it was something he had created for himself, by his own efforts and with his considerable intelligence. She wondered if he had chosen finance as a career because a balance sheet told its own unequivocal story, clear as the paper it was written on, without any messy emotion to blur the issues.

And then the steel in his eyes softened to warmth as he smiled. 'I hope you didn't mind me sending the car for you, Mirry.'

She shook her head, her smile widening as she remembered her fright. 'Though when he said you'd been delayed and he'd been sent to collect me, for some reason I assumed he'd be driving me all the way home. I nearly had a heart attack when he drove into the underground car park. I thought for a moment I was being kidnapped.'

He chuckled. 'Now, why do I think you'd take even that in your stride?' He noticed the secretary's raised eyebrows as she observed Mirry's diminutive size. 'Carol, I have it on the best authority that Mirry's stronger than she looks.'

Mirry laughed delightedly, surprised he had remembered, and nodded her agreement when he asked if she could give him just a few more minutes. Instantly he reverted to the decisive and, she suspected, demanding boss, listening to Carol's messages and issuing instructions. He picked up his bulging briefcase. 'I'm taking the Hong Kong figures with me to work on. Keir Minto was going to send someone to the house to install the new computer link today—he already has? Splendid. I'll put the results on tomorrow and you can give copies to the board.

'OK, Mirry, let's get out of here before something else turns up.' Barely giving her time to say goodbye to the two secretaries, he swept her out of the office and across to the lift. Minutes later the Jaguar was weaving through the traffic, making for the M1.

'Sorry about the delay,' he apologised, drawing up for a red light.

'Well worth it to travel home in this sort of comfort,' Mirry assured him. He was still wearing the same grey business suit, the sober tie still firmly in place, yet he seemed to have sloughed off his busy executive skin, the hard lines of his face relaxed.

The car moved again. 'You were very patient. Hope you weren't bored out of you mind.'

'Not a bit. In fact I was riveted. The first time I've had a glimpse of a tycoon at work.'

'Tycoon?' He pulled a self-deprecating face. 'I don't flatter myself I'm anywhere near John Shilbury's league.'

There was silence for a while. Jay was having to concentrate on the traffic and Mirry didn't want to distract him. But, when they finally reached the motorway and the car surged forward, Jay said suddenly, 'I was amazed that John Shilbury had even heard of my existence, let alone that he was prepared to acknowledge me. I always thought——'

'That you were a dark skeleton hidden away in David's cupboard?' Mirry finished. 'But you were the son he had always wanted, so why should he keep you a secret?' She gave him a quick glance. Always before when she'd tried to talk to him about his father, he'd resisted. Was he prepared to listen at last?

'Of course, I don't really remember the time when he and Georgie were still hoping to adopt you,' she said softly, 'but when I was a child your father talked about you often. He was so proud of you, showing the few photos he had of you around, boasting how well you were doing at school. I can remember how excited he got before one of his trips to London, and how unhappy he often was when he came back and told us he hadn't been able to see you, after all.' At Jay's raised eyebrows, she explained, 'I believe your mother often made difficulties.'

She saw him frown, but when he made no comment she went on, 'I was about ten or eleven when they re-decorated a study bedroom for you, and asked Dad to turn the vegetable garden into a tennis court. You were coming up to your eighteenth birthday, you see, grown up, and they thought you would be able to visit them at Wenlow without having to ask your mother's permission.'

She saw his hands tighten their grip on the steering wheel. 'And instead I told him I wanted nothing more to do with him.'

Did he regret that decision now? she wondered. It had hurt David badly, and, because he was hurt, Georgie was too. But, in case he was regretting it, she was compassionate enough not to tell him that.

Instead she said, 'He didn't talk about you as often, then, but he knew you got a good degree when you left university, and he knew about you going into banking. Only when you went abroad did he lose track. It took Mr Golding several days to trace you when David died so suddenly.'

There was silence for a while, then Jay said harshly, as if something was grating in his throat, 'You say I was the son my father always wanted, but can you say the same of his wife? Wasn't Lady Jayston more relieved than disappointed at not being called upon to give houseroom to her husband's bastard?'

'No!' Mirry denied that vehemently. 'She wanted whatever would make David happy. There was nothing small about Georgie, least of all her heart.' But she could tell from his expression that he didn't believe her.

She turned in her seat, tucking her legs up so she was facing him. 'Jay, why do you think Georgie was ready to embark on the upheaval of converting two-thirds of her home into flats... at her time of life and in her indifferent state of health?'

He shrugged. 'I've no idea.'

She was nettled at his apparent display of indifference, and decided to let him have the unvarnished truth. 'Because she couldn't bear to think that, having finally inherited what was rightfully yours, you'd have to sell because you couldn't afford to live there.'

Jay never took his eyes off the road, but she saw his jaw clench. 'That mattered to her?'

'It mattered. Because even though it had been your mother's demands over the years that left the estate in such a bad way financially, Georgie felt guilty.'

This time he darted her a frowning glance. 'What did *she* have to feel guilty about?'

'My own reaction entirely. She was just as much a victim of the situation as you were. But she felt that, because of David's love for her, she'd always stood between you and your father, between you and your rightful place at Wenlow. So she thought up the conversion scheme to make the house self-supporting, and intended to use her own money—which David had always refused to touch—to put the scheme into action. She wanted you at Wenlow. She wanted you to feel secure there, to feel you belonged. She wanted you to be part of the family. Does that sound like a woman who bore a grudge?'

At first he didn't respond, then she saw the grim lines of his profile relax. 'I don't know how it is, Miss Grey,' he said with a reluctant laugh, 'but you seem to turn every preconceived notion I've ever had on its head.'

Mirry relaxed too, recognising his tacit admission that he believed her. 'I can tell you about the history of Wenlow too, if you like. When I was about sixteen I helped your father go through the archives. Jaystons have lived at Wenlow for more than four hundred years.'

'You don't think all those highly respectable ancestors will be turning in their graves at a bastard stepping into their hallowed shoes?' he asked drily, and Mirry wondered if his illegitimacy still rankled.

She decided the best way of handling the question was to treat it lightly. 'I think "wrong side of the blanket" would be the term they'd use, and what makes you think they were all respectable? Some of the stories would curl your hair! Anyway, what difference does it make? You're no less of a Jayston by blood, and it's still *your* family history.'

This time the fleeting glance was amused. 'You should have taken up law, not architecture. You could convince any jury the most blackhearted villain was innocent. So, tell me some of my family history.'

Elated, Mirry spent the rest of the journey telling him of the first Jayston who had fought on the side of Henry Tudor at the Battle of Bosworth, and had been rewarded with the Manor of Wenlow, where he had built the original Hall that was now the Dower House. And how, in the sixteen hundreds, a Jacobean Jayston had built the present Hall, only to almost lose it by backing the Royalist side in the Civil War. She had reached the return of the heir on the restoration of Charles the Second when they drew up in the courtyard of the Dower House.

Jay lifted out her bag and, before she could thank him, her mother was at the door to greet them. 'Simon rang to tell me you were bringing Mirry home, Jay. Thank you. You must stay for dinner, of course. I insist,' she added, though Jay had made no sign he was about to turn the invitation down. 'I've already told Martha not to expect you till later.'

To Mirry's joy, he accepted with every appearance of pleasure. It had to mean he'd made no definite arrangement to see Annabel tonight, so she could enjoy the bittersweet pleasure of his company for a few more hours.

Nick volunteered to take Jay to one of the bathrooms to freshen up, asking eagerly after Tricia Charlesworth as they climbed the stairs. His speech had improved a lot in the weeks since Jay's arrival at Wenlow, and it brought home to Mirry once again that it was time she began to organise her own future.

Later, relaxing with a drink in front of the sitting-room fire because the evening had turned cool, Mirry managed to overcome her inertia to ask, 'Isn't it time we were serving up, Mum?'

Cathy glanced at the carriage clock on the mantel-piece. 'It won't hurt for a few more minutes. We're just waiting——' She broke off, turning towards the door. 'Oh, here they are now.'

And to Mirry's disconcerted confusion, Annabel Frost walked in. Her first thought was that she had been in-vited for Jay's benefit, but then Andrew followed her in, his bright blue eyes challenging Jay as he curved a proprietorial arm around Annabel's waist.

Anxiously, Mirry glanced at Jay as he rose to his feet to greet them, but his smile was warm and friendly, dis-playing neither surprise nor resentment. Annabel, too, though taken aback in the first few moments at finding herself face to face with the man she'd shown every sign of falling in love with only days ago, greeted him as though their friendship had never been more than platonic.

So it was a puzzled and preoccupied Mirry at the dinner-table that night, only showing a flash of her usual sparkle as she related the meeting between Jay and Lord Shilbury. Had Annabel been mistaken in her feelings for Jay? she wondered. And what about Jay? Was he putting a good face on it in the light of her apparent defection? Mirry knew very well how good he was at hiding his feelings.

But it wasn't until much later, when Mirry was walking him out to his car, that Jay himself brought the subject up, saying drily, 'It looks as if Annabel's decided to forgive Andrew at last.'

'You—you knew about that?'

'That he trod heavily on her feelings in the past? Yes, she told me.'

'And—and you don't mind? That she's turned back to him, I mean?'

'Should I?' He had moved closer, not touching, but close enough that she could feel his body heat.

'Well, I thought you must.' She moistened her dry lips. 'I was there when the two of you met, remember. It was instant attraction between you.'

In the light from the porch, something seemed to flare in his eyes. 'Were you jealous, Mirry?' he asked softly.

Colour burned her cheeks. 'It hurt,' she said honestly, 'when you made it so obvious you *disliked* me.'

Jay sighed. 'I'm ashamed to say I meant it to hurt.' And then, at the wounded look on her face, 'Oh, Mirry, you can't be *that* innocent. If we're talking about instant attraction, the air positively crackled every time we met. But you were a Grey, a member of the clan I'd been brought up to hate and resent. So instead of rushing you to the nearest bed and making passionate love to you— which is what I ached to do—I was as nasty to you as possible.'

Mirry's whole body was suddenly molten with heat. No man had ever spoken to her like that, and the images he had created in her mind made her dizzy. 'And do you still hate us—me?' she croaked.

His hands came up to fondle her shoulders, drawing her closer, and once again she experienced the sweet, heady intoxication of his kiss. 'Does it seem as if I hate you?' he whispered.

She shook her head, too breathless with wonder for words, and he laughed softly, as if pleased with the effect he was having on her emotions. 'Then why don't you come over to the Hall tomorrow? We can discuss that conversion plan of yours.'

'Y-you're going to stay, then?' She couldn't hide her eagerness.

He kissed her again lingeringly, then, putting her from him, got into the car, lowering the window to say smilingly, 'Let's say I'm open to persuasion. You'll come tomorrow?'

'Oh, yes...' she breathed. 'In the afternoon?'

Watching his receding tail-lights, Mirry could hardly believe how things had changed in just a few hours. Had Jay really implied that he'd been attracted to her all along? Could he really be feeling the same turbulent emotions that were turning her life upside-down?

She thought of Annabel's astonishing change of heart and frowned. He hadn't just said those things to save face, had he? No, hadn't he behaved last night as if he really did like her, after all, hadn't he even kissed her, and all before he knew Annabel was seeing Andrew?

When Annabel greeted her at the stables the next morning with, 'Did you have a nice time with Jay in London, then?' Mirry's doubts returned. Not for anything would she have her actions hurting someone else.

'Oh, Annabel...is *that* why you were with Andrew last night?' If Annabel had somehow known about it, then maybe *she* had been saving face, and that meant Andrew too could be hurt. 'Look, I wasn't trying...I mean, I *knew* how you felt about Jay, and I wouldn't——'

'Oh, that.' Oddly, Annabel looked embarrassed. 'I wish you'd forget about that, Mirry. Actually I made a bit of a fool of myself. And anyway, I didn't know about your date with Jay till you spoke about it last night. I—I'd already been out several times with Andrew.'

'To make Jay jealous?' Mirry asked anxiously.

'No!' Annabel's denial was emphatic. 'If the truth be known, I only went after Jay in the first place to make Andrew mad. Only, well, he *is* very attractive, all that cool authority. And I suppose I got a bit carried away. The thing is, Mirry, I knew all along I was getting nowhere, especially,' she pulled a rueful face, 'as he spent most of our time together asking about you.'

'Me?' Mirry was astounded.

'I know you thought he disliked you, but believe me, he was always talking about you. Don't worry.' Annabel gave a laughing shrug. 'It was only my pride that was hurt. And then, after Jay went back to London the last time, I bumped into Andrew by accident and... well, discovered I'd never really stopped loving him.'

Mirry's face lit with a delighted smile as she hugged the other girl. 'Oh, Annabel, I'm so glad! I love the idea of having you for a sister.'

Annabel coloured like a peony. 'Hey, we haven't got that far yet! We're only just getting to know each other again.' Her expression softened. 'But thanks for the sentiment.'

When Mirry took the path through the gardens to the Hall that afternoon it was with a feeling of acute nervous excitement, and where in the past she would have gone through the kitchen, she carried on round to the front, her nervousness increasing as she rang the bell.

A nervousness that seemed justified when Jay opened the door, frowning and demanding, 'What's all this in aid of?'

Had he forgotten? Mirry wondered, flustered. Had the warmth he'd shown her last night been a mirage? He was wearing jeans and a light cotton sweater, both garments displaying a well-muscled body and her awareness of him only increased her confusion. 'I—you asked me to come round this afternoon, if you remember.'

'Of course I remember!' And then, when she winced at his impatience, 'Did you always ring the doorbell when my father was alive?'

'No, of course not, but——'

'Then don't do it now.'

Her brow clearing as she realised the source of his impatience, Mirry allowed herself to be drawn inside, murmuring mischievously, 'No, sir, of course not, sir.'

'There's only one way to deal with that kind of insubordination.' Jay drew her closer, a smile softening his threat, and Mirry was sure he would have kissed her but for Martha Barks' breathless, 'Oh, you've seen to it, Mr Jay. I thought—Mirry! Why on earth were you ringing the doorbell?'

'I've just chastised her about that, Mrs Barks.' Jay turned to the housekeeper and the moment was gone, for when he took Mirry through to the library he was completely businesslike. At first, as she went over her plans with him, her feeling of disappointment made it hard to concentrate, but, by the time they were moving around the house so that he could visualise for himself how it would all work, her enthusiasm for the project took over.

'You see the east wing already has a separate entrance and staircase,' she pointed out, 'and splits perfectly into four flats, two one-bedroomed ones on the ground floor—ideal for a retired couple who don't want stairs—and two much larger flats upstairs. It will mean putting a staircase into each of them up to the attic floor, and knocking some dividing walls down in those attics to make three good-sized bedrooms.

'The west wing posed more problems as there's no staircase on that side of the house. But I got round that by making each floor a self-contained unit. Come and see what I mean.' She rushed him back through the main part of the house to the big formal drawing-room with french windows opening on to the terrace.

'I did think of making this the entrance to the ground floor flat, but it's such a lovely room I was reluctant to spoil it, so...' She took him through the french windows and round the back end of the wing where there was a window that almost reached ground level. 'I decided if that window came out and was replaced by a door...and that one too...' she pointed up at the first floor 'then build an *outside* staircase—the first and second floor flat would share the outer door, and in the hallway inside there's room for a stair up to the attic floor. Because of the size of the drawing-room, the ground floor will have only two bedrooms, but the other two floors will have three.' She took him inside again to show him how the layout would be.

Jay looked and listened, but made no comment until, as they came to the end of their tour, he asked, 'What about the main house?' And, at her puzzled look, 'I see you've made no plans for any alterations there to make up for the rooms it will lose.'

'But the wings haven't been used for years, except for the music-room, and very occasionally the drawing-room. You'll still have the library and dining-room, as well as the little sitting-room, with the hall for large-scale entertaining. And there'll still be the four main bedrooms—five if you turn Georgie's sitting-room into a bedroom, though I suppose that would only work if the adjoining room was a nursery.' She found herself blushing as she mentioned the nursery. 'Anyway, the main house is *your* concern. You must have your own ideas how you would like it.'

He seemed to be taking an inordinate interest in her flushed cheeks, and after a few moments said softly, 'Tell me, Mirry, are you a virgin?'

She flushed even redder until her fine skin burned, then, telling herself she had nothing to feel embarrassed about, lifted her chin challengingly. 'Yes,' she said. 'Are you?'

His mouth twisted into a wry smile. 'No.' Appropriately enough, they were descending the marble staircase that had been the scene of Mirry's first embarrassing meeting with Jay. Not that *he* was showing any embarrassment when he went on, 'I've always been too aware of the dangers of bringing an unwanted child into the world to be a womaniser, but I have had a couple of relationships, the first when I was at university...'

Mirry didn't want to hear, but, completely oblivious that these unasked-for revelations were hurting her, he steered her towards the library. 'We shared a flat for more than a year, and I saw it as a preliminary to sharing the rest of our lives. I was very young, of course, and possibly greener than most. When she took her first job she moved on to a new man.'

He had loved her, Mirry thought, and half her anguish was for his hurt, the rest for her own.

CHAPTER NINE

'THE SECOND woman in my life was when I was working in New York.' Jay ushered her to the sofa and bent to switch on the electric fire. 'And although the affair lasted for a couple of years, I knew right at the start she was a career girl with no ambitions to settle for domesticity, so when Alpha Hotels offered me a directorship and I came back to England, there were no bones broken on either side. What would you like to drink? Sherry?'

'I—thank you,' she answered automatically, while still wondering why he had been telling her all this. But, glancing at her watch, she was staggered to find it was almost seven o'clock. 'Do you mind if I cancel that drink? Mum will have the meal ready.'

'I'll phone and tell her you're eating with me.'

'Oh! But what about Martha? She won't——'

'Martha had her instructions first thing this morning.' He put the glass in her hand. 'And we *do* still have things to discuss. What's the number?'

Mirry told him, but if she expected that discussion was to be about the conversion plans, she was mistaken.

After they had gone into the dining-room, where Martha had left everything in the heated trolley so they could serve themselves, Jay disconcerted her by asking, 'Were you serious about never having slept with any of your boyfriends?'

Again she felt the betraying colour sweeping across her cheeks, but, hanging on to her poise, she answered obliquely, 'I assume "slept" is a euphemism, since I suppose sleeping is the last thing one does on such occasions.'

'You *suppose*?' She was striving valiantly to spoon up her soup, but could feel his gaze boring into her.

'I haven't even talked about it with a man before, let alone done it,' she admitted with a rush, and finally looked up to see him shaking his head. 'You don't believe me?'

'Oh, yes, I believe you. I was shaking my head in wonder.' He finished his soup and, collecting her empty bowl too, returned them to the trolley and began to serve Martha's delicious chicken casserole. 'Why? I mean, you can't have lacked opportunity. You're twenty-three years old, you lived away from home for two years, and with five brothers you can't have lacked admirers among their friends. So it has to be because that's the way you wanted it—or *didn't* want it in this case—because you're not going to tell me no man's ever been tempted to warm his hands, if not his heart, on a girl like you.'

It was an expression she hadn't heard before, and she wondered fleetingly if Jay wanted to warm his heart on her, or merely his hands. 'I can't answer your question, because I don't know myself,' she finally confessed. 'I suppose, having grown up with five brothers, boys were never quite as fascinating a subject to me as they were to my friends. And any dates I *did* have were very much aware of those brothers if they stepped out of line.'

Jay laughed. 'Yes, I can see they'd be a definite deterrent to the local lads. But what about when you were at university? There must have been more men than women on your course, and *they* wouldn't know you had five hulking brothers standing guard.'

'I was working too damned hard for those kind of distractions. And of course the last couple of years I've been busy with Nick.' Her eyes flicked to his face and away again. 'Or perhaps it was because I'd never met a man who—who made me feel...' She stumbled to a halt.

'Who made you feel like I do when I kiss you?' Jay suggested softly, and once again Mirry experienced the feeling of her whole body melting. He laughed softly. 'You can't deny it, Mirry. We both know the attraction's there, and has been ever since we first met. If it makes you feel any better about it, then I'll tell you it's never happened like this for me before, either.'

It surprised her into looking up at him, wide brown eyes meeting clear grey ones. 'H-hasn't it, Jay?' she whispered.

He shook his head. 'No, never.'

Her smile was so blindingly happy that he blinked, and his cutlery rattled against his plate. And when he said, 'I should have gone down to the cellar to see if there's some wine,' his voice sounded as if he didn't quite have control of it.

'Oh, there's racks of it down there,' Mirry told him happily. 'Your father laid down some rather good stuff when you were born, and I know there's some champagne that was meant for your twenty-first birthday.'

Jay looked so shaken, she was concerned.

'Are you all right?' He didn't answer and her hand crept over the table to touch his.

He gripped it hard. 'Ever since we met you've been telling me my father *did* care, yet it takes a silly little thing like knowing he laid wine down for me to really bring it home.'

'Oh, Jay...' Tears pricked her eyes as, her hand still in his, she slid out of her chair and came round the corner of the table, resting her free hand on his shoulder. 'He cared very much, and he never stopped caring. Why, even the history of Wenlow I helped him research was done for you, and that was after——' She broke off, hesitating to remind him it was at his own wish that he had broken all association with his father.

Jay was not so squeamish. 'After I turned my back on him,' he supplied sombrely. 'I really relished that, you know, rejecting him the way I thought he'd always rejected me. God, what a self-righteous little prig I was!'

The tears welled up in Mirry's eyes. With a groan he thrust his chair back, gathering her into his arms and kissing the moisture away. Her response began as a compassionate urge to comfort, but quickly flared into something much deeper and more demanding. Jay's kiss seemed to be searching for the very essence of her, as if he would draw it from her body into his. And she gave it willingly, vividly aware of his arousal and clinging to him as her only salvation as she launched herself into the uncharted seas of sexual love.

At first she thought the noise was the sound of her heart beating erratically, but as Jay finally drew away she realised it was the plopping of the coffee percolator. He didn't release her at once, but the nature of his embrace changed as he deliberately banked down the fires he had lit.

'I was going to suggest we took our coffee into the library,' he said, to Mirry's inexperienced eyes perfectly composed while she was still trembling. 'But I'm not sure that's a good idea.'

Mirry took a deep breath and tried to reason herself out of the let-down feeling. 'Maybe I should go home now,' she said shakily.

'Hey, you don't have to be afraid of me.' His hands slid down her arms to clasp her hands. 'I think I've learned enough self-control over the years. We'll go into the library and you can show me this history you and my father drew up.'

Mirry went happily, too shy to tell him fear wasn't at all the emotion he aroused in her.

Over the next three weeks Mirry saw a lot of Jay. He had to spend some of his time in London, but back in Wenlow after each trip he immediately sought her out. She talked to him about his father, painting vivid word pictures for the son who had barely known him; she took him around the estate and surrounding countryside, introducing him to everyone, not only tenants on the estate and in the tiny village, but the owners of some of the larger nearby houses. Yet the only comment he had made on her plans for the conversion had been that the way she had solved some of the problems was ingenious. Several times Mirry was on the point of asking if he meant to go ahead; only the fear that he might think she was angling for the job held her back.

But, if Mirry was diffident of probing Jay's thinking, that galvanic attraction still sizzled between them, though he was much better at banking it down then she was. In fact he never asked her to dine alone with him at the Hall again, but always made sure there were others present. Night after night she would lie alone in her bed, unbearably aroused by his kisses, sometimes feeling angry with him for his control, yet knowing in her heart of hearts that he was exercising it for her protection. And, if her parents were beginning to look perturbed at the amount of time Mirry and Jay were spending together, Mirry herself was far too absorbed in all these new emotions to notice.

And then one day Mirry returned from a session at the riding stables with the handicapped children to be greeted by her mother with, 'Jay rang. He's had to rush off to Birmingham and wants you to look after some people he's expecting at the house.'

In the process of shrugging off her coat, Mirry immediately pulled it back on again and would have rushed straight over to the Hall if her mother hadn't said drily, 'They're not arriving till after lunch so you do have time to eat.'

'I'll have to change too,' Mirry said, glancing down at her worn jeans and baggy sweater. 'I wonder who these people are?'

Watching her daughter's vivid face, Cathy Grey's uneasiness grew, but even as she opened her mouth to voice her fears Mirry had whisked out of the kitchen and up the stairs.

The morning had been cloudy and cool, but by early afternoon the sky had cleared and the sun made a nimbus of light in Mirry's reddish-brown curls as she stood in the library window. The cotton dress she had changed into was almost the exact pink of the 'candles' on the chestnut trees around the little church, but Mirry was too busy wondering about the expected guests to notice. Jay hadn't mentioned them last night when they had dined with the Mintos, so she guessed it must have been a last-minute arrangement and was pleased and flattered that he had asked her to stand in for him.

At last she saw a car turn in at the gate and hurried to the front door. The car was not one she recognised, and the middle-aged man climbing out of the driver's seat was a stranger too. Mirry started down the steps then stopped, staring at the young woman emerging from the other side of the car. 'Kate! Kate Redding!' she exclaimed. 'What on earth are you doing here?'

'Mirry!' Kate mirrored her surprise. 'I was about to ask you the same thing. I thought this was the house Jay recently inherited.'

'Yes, it is,' Mirry laughed. 'He had to dash off to Birmingham and asked me to be here to welcome you. I wish he'd told me it was you I was waiting for, though.' She turned apologetically to the man who had been listening to their exchange, and missed Kate's raised eyebrows.

'This is Clive Summers, Mirry.'

Before Kate could finish the introduction, the man said peevishly, 'We'll never get back to London tonight at this rate,' and reached into the car to take out a large sketch-block.

Taken aback by his lack of courtesy, Mirry still managed a politely apologetic, 'I'm sorry, but I really don't know when Jay will be back.'

He dismissed her with, 'No matter. I prefer to do the initial survey alone,' and marched straight past her into the house.

'You mustn't mind Clive,' Kate said as Mirry stared after him. 'He thinks his genius absolves him from common politeness. And he *is* a genius, though it grieves me to admit it.'

Even more at sea, Mirry asked, 'A genius at what?'

'His job, of course. He's a director of Wren Interiors and I'm supposed to be his assistant, though half the time he insists he works better alone.' Kate grimaced. 'I think he only brought me along to read the map.'

Mirry had forgotten that Kate worked for the interior design firm and a cold, hollow feeling was developing in the pit of her stomach. 'You'd better come in, Kate.' She led the way through the echoing hall, waiting until they reached the library to ask, 'But what has he come here to do?'

'Hasn't Jay told you? He's had this idea of converting part of the house into luxury flats and has asked us to do a preliminary survey.' Kate looked concerned as Mirry sat down rather suddenly. 'I say, are you all right?'

Mirry hardly heard her. At least her worst fear wasn't to be realised. Jay *wasn't* intending to turn the house over to Alpha Hotels before disappearing back to London. But, if he was going ahead with the flats scheme, why had he brought in someone else? He'd already told her she had solved some of the problems ingeniously. It could only mean that he didn't think she was capable of seeing the job through. That hurt, but what hurt even more was that he hadn't told her what he was planning. Over the last few weeks she had thought they'd grown really close, yet he had gone behind her back and then let her learn the truth in a way that was almost callous.

'Mirry...' Kate's voice finally penetrated. 'I've upset you, haven't I? I don't know how, but I can see——'

'Not you, Kate.' Mirry pulled herself together and even managed a wan smile. 'It was just rather a shock...'

Kate frowned. 'Jay's plans for the house, you mean?'

'Not exactly. I knew about those before Jay ever inherited Wenlow, because I drew them up myself.'

'*You* did?' Kate's eyes rounded.

'Well, it was Aunt Georgie—Lady Jayston's idea. She realised that once death duties were paid, the estate wouldn't bring in enough for the upkeep of the house. The flats were her idea to make the house self-supporting. And when I showed the plans to Jay he seemed to like them.'

She broke off as she saw the expression on Kate's face, a mixture of scepticism and embarrassment.

'Oh, Kate, I'm not accusing you of stealing the job from me, don't think that. If I'm honest, I can't blame Jay for calling in the professionals. Just two years of a seven-year architecture course hardly gives me the qualifications or the expertise of a firm like yours.' Her voice wavered, betraying her hurt. 'But he could have told me, not left me to find out like this.'

'Indeed he should!' Kate agreed, privately wondering just how deeply the little redhead had got herself involved. 'But the fact that he didn't doesn't surprise me, Mirry.' She hesitated, then went on awkwardly, 'There's a great deal to admire in Jay, but his least endearing characteristic is his blind spot where the feelings of others are concerned. It's as if he's never learned to consider how any action of his might affect someone else, which isn't really surprising when nobody's ever cared a damn for him—except possibly my mother-in-law. And Steven, my husband. They first became friends at prep school. Mirry, you wouldn't believe some of the horror stories Steven told me about Jay's childhood, abandoned by his father and ignored by his mother.'

'His father *didn't* abandon him!' Mirry leapt at once to David's defence. 'Believe me, if he'd had the slightest inkling of the real state of affairs, he'd have got custody somehow.'

Kate flushed uncomfortably. 'Oh, crumbs! I'd forgotten you knew him.'

'Even Jay's convinced now that he was wrong about his father all these years,' Mirry declared.

'Well, if that's so, I can only be glad about it.' Kate sighed. 'But don't you see, it doesn't really change the effect the absence of love and affection had on the formation of Jay's personality, making him the man he is today?'

Mirry was silenced because she could see the truth of that, and when Kate, even more ill at ease, went on to say, 'Jay would be a dangerous man for any woman to fall in love with,' she knew the other girl was warning her.

She knew, too, that the warning was too late. She was already fathoms deep in love with him; even the way he had hurt her today didn't change that. If someone had warned her right at the beginning, she wasn't sure it would have made any difference, because something in Jay called to something in her, something above and beyond the strong physical attraction.

'Don't you think it's time someone *did* begin to teach him about love?' she suggested quietly. But Kate only shook her head, more in pity than in denial.

And then Kate said briskly, 'Will you show me round the house, Mirry? I mean all of it, not just the wings.'

Mirry agreed promptly, glad to get away from the subject of her relationship with Jay.

'It's not often you find a house of this age still furnished as it was originally,' Kate said appreciatively as Mirry showed her the formal drawing-room. 'I gather you know this house well. How do you feel about it being split up?'

'I think it's a great idea,' Mirry said at once. 'Several big houses around here have been completely split up into several units, but Aunt Georgie didn't want that. By only converting the wings, Jay's still left with a good-sized house to live in himself.'

'Jay *is* intending to live here, then?' Kate looked sceptical. 'Rather a long way from London, I'd have thought.'

'Well, as you said yourself, he plays his cards close to his chest, but we *are* convenient for motorways here, and Jay's already installed a computer which keeps him in touch with his office.'

'Hmm, I noticed it.' Kate dropped the subject, only talking about the house and its décor as they continued the tour.

'You're not making any notes,' Mirry commented curiously. 'And surely one afternoon isn't long enough for your boss to take all the necessary measurements.'

'Oh, this is only a preliminary visit, just to get the feel of the place. Clive at least will have to spend some time here later, and perhaps he'll want me along too. Though, as you know, I hate having to leave my kids.'

'If you *do* come, why don't you stay at the Dower House with us?' Mirry suggested diffidently. 'It's only a short walk through the grounds. Then you could bring the twins with you.'

Kate's mouth dropped open. 'Do you really mean that?'

'Of course. Mum and I would love to look after them while you're working. And if it coincides with Simon's leave,' she added with sly mischief, 'we could get him down here, too.'

Colour flared in Kate's cheeks. 'I suppose you know I've been seeing him?'

'He did mention it,' Mirry grinned.

'Well, many thanks for the offer, but we'll have to see, won't we?' Kate was doing her best to sound casual, but Mirry noticed her eyes were very bright.

They had reached the principal bedrooms by now, and Kate lingered beside one of the four-poster beds, fingering the hangings. 'You know, I've never seen such a collection of Jacobean needlework, and all in perfect condition, too.'

Mirry had noticed Kate taking a particular interest in the embroideries throughout the tour. 'They are now,' she laughed, 'but you should have seen them a few years ago, before Aunt Georgie and I started restoring them.'

'*You* did work like this?' Kate stared at her. 'But where did you learn to do it?'

'By trial and error,' Mirry admitted. 'We just copied the patterns and practised until we felt competent enough to actually work on the originals. It's taken us ten years, and there are still two small chairs waiting for attention.'

'Ten years? But that makes you an expert,' Kate said excitedly. She indicated the bed curtains. 'How much of this is your repair work?'

'A fair bit. This one had perished along the folds, which is why we left the curtains hanging down instead of looping them back,' Mirry explained.

'But can you show me which is your work and which is original?'

Mirry looked doubtful. 'Not without taking off the lining.' And when Kate looked incredulous, she went on, 'It really wasn't difficult, once we'd found someone to dye the yarns the exact shades, because the patterns here were still mostly complete. One of the other beds had one curtain that was showing very little pattern, and the sofa I finished just before Jay came here had no pattern at all. I had to start from scratch and design my own.'

'You do upholstery, too? You really are a dark horse!' Mirry shook her head, laughing. 'Mirry, haven't you any idea how impossible it is to find people with your knowledge and skills? I'll tell you now, Graham Wren would offer you a job with us on the strength of that alone, and look on your knowledge of architecture as a bonus.'

Mirry was astonished, regarding her deftness with a needle as a very minor talent. 'You're not serious?'

'Indeed I am.' Kate hesitated. 'Look, I don't know whether you were intending to go back to architecture, but if you're interested in switching to interior design, I'm quite certain Graham would jump at the chance of taking you on.'

Mirry was speechless, her mind whirling. Here was just the exciting career opportunity she'd been looking for, so why was she hesitating? Because it would mean leaving Wenlow, of course. No, why not be completely honest? Because it would mean leaving Jay and whatever it was that had been growing between them.

Yet hadn't Jay shown her plainly enough by his actions today how mistaken she had been in thinking his feelings were as strong as her own? Wouldn't it be wiser to take this job, put a distance between them before she got herself in too deep to recover? But then, when did love ever listen to wisdom?

While she was still torn by indecision, Kate said, 'Mirry, at least let me tell Graham about you. If you don't want a full-time job, you might be able to take on certain projects working from home. And it wouldn't do you any harm going to talk to him.'

And Mirry had to agree.

She was giving Kate and Clive tea in the library when the snarl of an exhaust outside heralded Jay's return. Mirry's cup rattled against the saucer, and she took a deep breath to try to settle her bouncing heart. Her eyes on the door, she saw his first glance was for her, then he was smoothly greeting the visitors.

'Mirry's looking after you, I see.' Then, still without a word of apology or explanation to Mirry, 'Well, Clive, what do you think?'

'A challenge, but that's what I thrive on.' Clive swept a hand theatrically through his over-long grey hair. 'It'll mean a lot more structural alteration than it would have done if you'd stuck to your original idea of turning the place into a hotel, but I have no doubt I can come up with the right scheme.'

Mirry winced and wondered what structural alterations the man intended. Her own scheme had entailed very few. She found she couldn't look at Jay, her hurt at his thoughtless treatment of her reanimated as she listened to the conversation.

Then Clive was saying, 'Time we were off, Kate. I'll let you know when it's convenient for me to come down for a few days.'

Kate's spluttered giggle at the man's pomposity was hurriedly changed to a cough, but Mirry didn't find it at all amusing. She was only too aware that in a few moments she would be alone with Jay, and she hadn't made up her mind yet what she was going to say to him.

Kate rather limited her options when she called out as she was getting into the car, 'I'll be in touch, Mirry, just as soon as I've spoken to Mr Wren.'

Jay glanced at her sharply, but waited until the car was pulling away before asking, 'What was all that about . . . Kate getting in touch?'

And because his behaviour towards her today still rankled she said bluntly, 'She's offered me a job. At least, she seems certain her boss will jump at the chance to employ me.'

'A job?' Jay looked stunned. 'You mean you're actually planning to leave here and work in London? But why? Not because of those stupid remarks of mine when we first met, I hope. You know I didn't——'

'Not entirely,' Mirry broke in, 'but I always intended finding something to do once Nick was better. It didn't seem so urgent while there was the chance you might want me to work on the flat conversions, but now Wren Interiors are going to do it . . . well, I won't be needed here.' To her horror, she felt tears pricking at her eyes.

The urge to cry got worse when Jay, looking completely baffled, said, 'You thought I'd want *you* to do the conversion?'

'Since you seemed to like the plans I'd drawn up, yes.' She blinked furiously to keep the tears at bay.

'But it never crossed my mind,' he admitted.

'I know that—*now*. It was brought home to me painfully.' She saw him frown. Kate was right. Strong, self-assured, successful, heart-wrenchingly attractive he might be, but he really had no idea how much he had hurt her today.

'I never meant to upset you.' His uncertainty now made it hard not to forgive him anything. 'And I didn't mean to imply you couldn't do the job successfully. I wanted Wren Interiors to do the flats so you could concentrate on the house itself once we're married.'

'Married?' There seemed no end to this man's capacity for surprising her. Of course, it was what she had secretly been dreaming about, hoping for, but the manner of his proposal left her speechless.

'It's what we were working up to, wasn't it? At least *I* was, until you slapped me down with this job idea.' It was that uncertainty again that was so appealing in a man usually so sure of himself.

Thrilled and delighted, Mirry threw herself into his arms. 'Oh, Jay, I do love you so...'

'You mean, you will? Marry me, I mean?'

She could feel the tension in him as she curled her arms lovingly round his neck, breathing, 'Oh, yes, Jay. Yes, please...'

With a groan he gathered her to him, lifting her right off the floor. 'Mmm, you're so tiny...so dainty...so warm...' Kisses punctuated his words. 'You fascinated me right from the start.' His warm breath in her ear made her shudder with delight. 'No more talk of leaving to get a job?'

She shook her head, smiling blissfully. 'There's only one job I want, being your wife.'

He lowered her feet to the floor, but only so he could unbutton the front of her dress and push it from her shoulders. Her back arched in helpless ecstasy as his mouth closed over the aroused nipple, moistening it through her silk teddy. Frantically she scrabbled at the buttons of his shirt, surrendering to the yearning to touch him as she had only touched him in her dreams before.

Her senses delighted in the crispness of his body hair against her fingertips, the suddenly accelerated thud of his heart against her palms, and she found it both touching and erotic the way she could make him tremble.

His voice was harsh and uneven as he groaned, 'Mirry...my little miracle...I want you in my home, in my bed, soon...'

The touch of his hands, the touch of his mouth, the erotic image his words conjured in her mind, and Mirry was lost. If he'd taken her there on the floor of the library it would have been with her full co-operation. It was Jay who, breathing raggedly, drew back, leaving her dazed and bereft.

'No, we mustn't,' he said hoarsely. 'Mirry, I want everything perfect, a virgin bride and a proper wedding night. Only it will have to be soon. No long engagement.'

Mirry was so touched, her eyes swam. 'Let's go and tell the family.' She smiled through her happy tears. 'Your family now, Jay.'

They took the path through the grounds, making for the kitchen where Mirry knew her parents would be together, talking over their day as her mother prepared the evening meal. She didn't notice the glance they exchanged as she burst into the kitchen, dragging Jay behind her, so she was entirely unprepared when her excited, 'Mum...Dad...Jay and I have just got engaged to be married,' was met with an appalled silence.

Confused, she glanced from one to the other. 'What's the matter? I—we thought you'd be pleased...'

Cathy Grey put down the spoon she was holding and pushed the saucepan to the back of the stove. 'Oh, darling...are you really sure about this?'

'Of course I am, Mum. I——'

Before she could tell them how much she loved him, Jay broke in, his face a wooden mask, 'Perhaps your parents don't care for you to marry a bastard.'

Donald Grey pushed himself out of his chair and said vehemently, 'That has nothing to do with it, son.'

'As if we'd let *that* make any difference,' Cathy echoed, visibly distressed at the construction Jay had put on her reservations. 'Truly, Jay, we have no personal objections to you at all. It's just that...' She looked uncomfortable, glancing at her husband for support.

'The fact is, Cathy and I have seen this coming and it's worried us,' Donald said heavily. 'Your mother won't like it, Jay.'

It was then that Mirry remembered Simon's joking remark about her parents not caring for the idea of Valerie Elphick as her mother-in-law, and her heart sank even further.

'I don't like to speak ill of her to you, Jay,' Cathy put in earnestly, 'but she stirred up so much trouble, the few months she was here, that we can't help fearing for Mirry.'

Mirry glanced at Jay apprehensively, and felt a measure of relief to see his wooden expression had relaxed. 'And that's your only objection?' he asked, his voice clipped. Her parents nodded, albeit uncertainly. 'Then I can assure you your fears are groundless.'

When her parents continued to look doubtful, he curved a possessive arm round Mirry's shoulders, drawing her closer. 'In the first place I like to think I can protect Mirry from anything unpleasant, and in the second place my mother sold up and went to California soon after I started at university. We corresponded sporadically for the first year, and the last I heard she was getting married. As she never replied to my letter wishing her well, I can only suppose she decided to break all contact with me. I don't know her married name, where she lives, or even if she's still alive, so it's hardly likely she'll decide to look me up after all this time, do you think?'

'But you were only eighteen when you went to university,' Cathy gasped, horrified. 'And she left you to fend for yourself?'

Jay shrugged. 'I'd been more or less fending for myself most of my life, Mrs Grey. I can't say I lost any sleep over it.'

'Cathy. You must call me Cathy...' Pink-cheeked, she glanced at her husband '...as you're going to be a member of the family.'

Mirry relaxed against Jay as the tension drained away, her face as she lifted it to smile at him radiant. There was a flurry of hugs and handshakes and wishes for their future, then Cathy said, 'We'll have to throw an engagement party, though it might have to be delayed until all the boys are free at the same time.'

'Just as long as you don't expect the wedding to be delayed,' Jay said firmly. 'We don't want a long engagement.'

'We thought a month, Mum,' Mirry concurred happily, then, seeing her mother's dismay added quickly, 'William and Eleanor were married within a few weeks of their engagement.'

'Yes, but they'd known each other a long time, while you and Jay...'

'Oh, Mum!' Mirry wailed. 'It's not as if we've got to save up to buy a house.'

'We have one that badly needs Mirry's talents to make it into a home,' Jay said, then, with an open appeal to her father, added 'And quite frankly, sir, though we'd both prefer to wait for our wedding night, I can't answer for the control of either of us if we're forced to wait.'

Mirry looked pleadingly at her parents, her cheeks peony-red. 'It's true. We love each other so much...'

Not for a moment did it occur to her to question that assertion.

CHAPTER TEN

EVERYONE declared it was the prettiest wedding the tiny Wenlow church had seen in years. The June day was perfect, with the sun pouring down and only a gentle breeze to ruffle the exotic hats. The bride in her white lace and fluffy veil was incandescent with happiness, while her groom displayed all the pride and protective possessiveness that was thought proper.

The five Grey brothers, immaculate in their morning suits, made impressive ushers. Of course the bride's side of the church far outstripped the groom's, but the church was so small and so packed with well-wishers that every seat was taken.

And the four little bridesmaids behaved like angels: Richard's two daughters and Kate Redding's twins. For when Simon had come home for the engagement party, he had brought Kate and her children with him.

Kate had been a little embarrassed, joining in the engagement celebrations so soon after warning Mirry against falling in love with Jay, but, warmed by the reception the Grey family extended to herself, and relieved and touched by their delight in her twin daughters, she soon forgot her unease.

For Mirry the last month had passed in a whirl: first the trip into Leicester to buy the engagement ring, an emerald flanked by two diamonds the size of which even now took her breath away, then the rush to see the vicar to put up the banns. There was the wedding gown to choose and the little girls to organise for fittings, not to mention Mirry's going-away outfit and the new beachwear she would need for the honeymoon on the Algarve where Lord Shilbury was loaning them his villa. But most exciting of all was going round the house with Jay, deciding what alterations they would need to do.

The old-fashioned kitchen would have to be completely gutted, of course. The whole place needed redecorating too, Jay declared, but that would have to wait until the new heating system had been installed, and at least two new bathrooms provided.

Mirry laughingly protested that maybe he was being too ambitious. 'It's going to cost an arm and a leg to do all that as well as going ahead with the conversion of the wings, Jay. Wouldn't we be better to do the house a little at a time as we can afford it?'

'I'd rather get all the upset over at once, then we can settle down in comfort.' He smiled at the anxious line creasing her brow. 'Am I getting myself a thrifty little wife? Don't worry, darling, if I run out of cash there's always Lady Jayston's legacy to fall back on. I still feel uncomfortable about accepting that anyway when——'

'But you need that to pay for the work on the new flats,' Mirry pointed out, but Jay just laughed.

'The flats are a business proposition—a good one, too. I had no trouble raising the finance. If there's one thing I know about, it's money, and if I have any talent, it's for making it. So anything you want to do in the house, anything you need to buy, go right ahead and get the best. I promise you won't bankrupt me.'

Of course Mirry had recognised at their first meeting that Jay wasn't the humble bank clerk of their imagining. She had known she was marrying a successful man, but this was the first intimation she had had that she was marrying a rich one.

So she had drawn up her plans for the house with the heady sensation of having a bottomless purse to draw on. Not that she was wantonly extravagant. The red brocade curtains at the library windows had rotted in the sun and would definitely have to be replaced, but the velvet in the dining-room had matured to a soft moss green and she decided to keep them.

There had been no time to put these plans into operation and have everything completed before the wedding, but at least they'd made a start on the most important part. For the last week Martha had been staying in the Dower House and Jay had been back in his London flat—which he had decided to keep on—while the builders and plumbers had moved in, promising the remodelled kitchen and the new heating system at least would be finished by the time they returned from their three-week honeymoon. Mirry had her doubts, but she was already looking forward to their return, to making a home for Jay and any children they might have.

And as he slipped the broad gold band on to her finger she looked up into his serious face, silently vowing that it would be a happy home, that he would find himself so loved he would forget all the years when it seemed no one cared.

At the reception in a marquee on the Dower House lawn a slimline Abby Minto—her precious new son left for the afternoon with the devoted Mrs Jameson—said, 'Oh, wouldn't David and Georgie have been pleased at this marriage!' And David's old friend, Lord Shilbury, heartily agreed. Wasn't everyone commenting on how Jay couldn't take his eyes off his radiant bride?

They cut the three-tiered wedding cake, drank the toasts, Jay responding wittily to the speeches, and when it was time for them to change they slipped upstairs hand in hand. On the wide landing, away from the prying eyes, they paused before going to their separate rooms, just looking at each other.

Jay's hand came out to touch the froth of veiling round Mirry's head and whispered unsteadily, 'You take my breath away.'

'Oh, Jay...' Deeply touched, Mirry's dark eyes brimmed with tender loving. 'We're going to be so happy...I promise...'

She believed it implicitly, and even if she had remembered Kate's warning of the irreversible forces that had formed Jay's personality she would still have believed it.

In a cotton voile dress, the colour subtly shading from gold to flame, the finely pleated skirt flaring as she moved, she looked like a flame herself, dancing lightly round her encircling family saying her farewells, Jay sticking proprietorially by her side.

They had hoped to slip away through the grounds to the Hall, where Jay had left his car with their luggage safely locked in the boot, but of course family and guests streamed after them, and though they were spared the usual 'Just Married' messages scrawled on the car, as they drove away from the laughing crowd a rattling din followed them.

'Your brothers!' Jay exclaimed, drawing into the first farm gateway along the lane to rid them of the unwelcome parting gift.

Mirry laughingly reminded him, 'They're your brothers too, now.'

Jay grimaced. 'If you say so. It'll take some getting used to.'

They were spending their wedding night at Jay's flat in London and flying out to Portugal the following day. The flat was in an imposing block in the Barbican with an underground car park and tight security. It was the first time Mirry had been there, and she was astonished at the understated luxury.

The sitting-room and the sunken dining area reached by two wide steps were decorated in shades of bronze and cream, the sofa and chairs upholstered in the softest bronze suede, the dining-table and two coffee-tables of heavy glass. Jay's bedroom was even more masculine, the predominating colour brown, while the second bedroom was furnished as a study with yet another computer brooding on the desk. There were two good-sized bathrooms, one with a bath large enough for two people and which she later discovered to have a whirlpool, but the kitchen was unexpectedly small, and, though well-equipped, looked as if it was rarely used.

With their plans for the house in mind, Mirry asked if he had done the décor himself, but Jay shook his head. 'I bought this place when I came back from New York. I was far too busy getting into the new job to bother with such things, so I turned it over to Wren Interiors.'

It was unreasonable, but she felt a stab of jealousy and asked, 'Did Kate do it?'

'I wanted a bachelor pad, not a boudoir,' he derided. Having shown her round, he carried her overnight case into the bedroom.

'Chauvinist,' she teased, following him, then was stuck by an unwelcome idea, her eyes drawn to the big bed.

'And did any of the ladies of your bachelor days share this with you?'

He moved towards her. 'Does it matter?'

He had already taken off his jacket and was now removing his tie. Mirry's heart began to bounce about in her breast. 'I—well, I know it shouldn't. I mean, what you did before we met...' His hands were fondling her shoulders, sliding beneath the material of her dress, and she was losing the thread of what she was trying to say.

He kissed her just below her ear, murmuring, 'I told you, I left the last lady back in New York. Now, how does this pretty thing come off?'

For a moment there was that flare of jealousy again as she imagined that New York lady sharing similar intimacies with Jay, and then, as the zip slid down and her dress pooled to the floor, the delicious, wondrous things he was doing and the promise of even more wondrous things to come drove everything else from her mind.

She was a little shy to be naked before a man for the first time in her life, her instinct to cover herself with her hands, but Jay soon found more exciting things for those hands to do, helping him undress. There was a moment when she trembled, the age-old virgin shrinking from the aroused male, until, drawn into something stronger than fear, she touched him. He gasped, and the fires they had deliberately banked down for the last four weeks burst into a conflagration.

At first she kept pace with him, mindless with delight at the feel of skin on skin, of his hands and mouth exploring, arousing, her slender body innocently inciting as it arched for closer contact, but then there was pain, and though a new pleasure followed she knew instinctively that he was outstripping her, convulsing into a pleasure that still eluded her before collapsing against her breasts.

'I'm sorry,' he gasped. 'God, I behaved as if *I* was the virgin!' He kept his face hidden as if he was ashamed, and he sounded shaken as he added, 'I've never lost control before.'

And although Mirry still felt as if she had had the gates of paradise slammed in her face, a wave of tenderness engulfed her. Her hands caressing the skin tautly stretched over his muscular back, she said, 'Then I take it as a compliment, darling.'

He did raise his head then, and she saw the shamed uncertainty in his eyes. 'But you didn't——' he began.

Because she didn't want their first time together to be marred in any way in his memory, she suggested quickly, 'No, but don't you think that was my lack of experience?' A mischievous smile danced in her brown eyes. 'Something that's in your power to remedy, and my teachers always told me I was a quick learner.'

He raised himself on his elbows to look into her face. 'Did they, indeed? Wait there.' He rolled off the bed and disappeared into the bathroom, and moments later Mirry heard water gushing. She lay there, her imagination savouring the male perfection of his naked body, but as the minutes passed curiosity was about to prompt her out of bed to see what was delaying him when he was back, scooping her up into his arms, carrying her through the door and lowering her into a bath full of scented water that boiled and churned with what she discovered to be a delicious sensation. And then he was in the water beside her, soaping her body with a suds-laden sponge and the sensation was even more delicious.

Just when the sponge was lost and his hands took over
she could never afterwards remember, but by the time
he lifted her out and wrapped her in a fluffy towel her
senses were heightened almost painfully. Shrugging into
a bathrobe himself, he set about caressing her dry: her
breasts, her belly, her hips, her thighs, spiralling the
sexual tension higher and higher until she shook like a
leaf. Then he discarded the towel, kneeling at her feet,
his hands firm against her hips, drawing her forward
until his face was buried against her sweet womanhood.

For a few moments shock made her resist the ir-
resistible, then, clinging to his shoulders for support, she
gave herself up to a convulsion of the most exquisite
sensation as she had never even imagined.

She cried out aloud as Jay raised his head, meeting
her glazed incredulity with open triumph. Then, as her
legs buckled beneath her, he was sweeping her up to carry
her back to bed, where for a few minutes he just held
her. Before the echoes of her ecstasy had quite died away,
his hands and mouth incited her again. And, having
tasted such delight once, her body demanded it again,
responding with an incitement of its own. This time there
was no pain, but a feeling of completion, each slow thrust
welcomed eagerly, each apparent withdrawal resisted as
she tightened instinctively to hold him. Hers was the
urgency now, every nerve in her body concentrating on
the rising tension until her world exploded into wave after
wave of sensation, making the pleasure she had experienced in the bathroom a mere foretaste.

It was some time before she could get control of her
sobbing breath. When she could, she asked diffidently,
'Did you——?'

Jay laughed, his breathing as ragged as her own. 'Didn't you notice?'

She shook her head. 'I was too...*astonished* by the wonderful things happening to me.'

She had certainly banished all sign of uncertainty in those silvery-grey eyes; instead there was only exultation. He rolled over on his side, carrying her suddenly boneless body with him. 'You incredible girl!' He chuckled into her ear. 'And your teachers were quite right.'

'Oh?' she questioned sleepily.

'You *are* a quick learner.'

And eager, too, for whether it was in a shady spot on the villa's private beach, or while the rest of the Algarve was sleeping away the hottest part of the day, or during the warm, starlit nights, Mirry's eagerness to learn was only matched by Jay's willingness to teach. They swam and sunbathed and made love, they took boat trips and sightseeing tours and made love, they dined out and danced and made love. In fact, it was everything a honeymoon should be—perfect—except for one small thing. Jay told her she was incredible, that she fascinated him. He told her how exciting she was, how much he wanted her, even whispered in her ear the things he was going to do to her which made her shudder with anticipation. But he never actually said he loved her.

Mirry told him she loved him several times a day, not only when they were making love, but across the table in a restaurant, sitting beside him on a crowded bus, shopping for souvenirs, and he would smile, his eyes gleaming in the way she recognised as a signal that he wanted to take her to bed, but he never responded with the words. She told herself it didn't matter, that it was his upbringing that was inhibiting him, that when he was more accustomed to their closeness it would loosen his tongue, that the words didn't really matter anyway when his actions were so loving. But it didn't stop her waiting for the response she wanted, or soften her disappointment when he stayed silent.

It wasn't until their last night at the villa that Mirry discovered why she was waiting in vain. She was taking her contraceptive pill as usual in the bathroom when Jay said, 'I wish you'd stop taking those things, Mirry.'

She looked at him through the mirror. 'I didn't know you wanted to start a family right away,' she said shyly.

He took the glass from her hand, turning her to face him. The idea of bearing his child was melting her inside, and she waited expectantly for him to say, I want *your* child, Mirry. But instead he said baldly, 'I want sons.' He gave a self-deprecating shrug. 'Funny, I never expected to feel this way, but then, I never expected to be my father's heir, either. Now...well, I find I have this urge to keep the line going, even if it is...what's the expression?...the bar sinister, and they'll be Elphicks, not Jaystons.'

Mirry slid her arms round his neck, happily believing it was their marriage that had brought about this change. 'You might find yourself with a quiver full of daughters,' she teased. 'Medical science hasn't perfected ordering a specific sex yet.'

Her happiness would have been complete if he'd assured her, 'As long as they all take after you, darling,' but her husband seemed to be working from a different script. He laughed the possibility aside. 'When you're the only girl in a family of five brothers? Hardly likely, I think.'

Mirry went cold. Surely he didn't mean...but he must know...it was never a secret... Her thoughts churned chaotically. And yet how would he know if no one had ever told him? And who would think to tell him something so apparently irrelevant? Why, she had almost forgotten it herself, the fact that the Greys' 'Little Miracle' was an adopted daughter.

Pulling away from Jay's arms, Mirry lurched into the bedroom, sinking on to the edge of the bed before her wobbly knees let her down. Puzzled, Jay followed and stood watching her from the doorway. She tried to speak and had to lick her dry lips and try again before she could ask the question branded into her brain. 'Is—is that why you married me? Because a girl with five brothers should be able to produce the sons you want?'

He hesitated, frowning at her white face and the intensity of her question before admitting, 'One of the reasons, yes.'

She bowed her head, her hair falling forward to hide her stricken face. 'And the other reasons?' It was like speaking through shards of glass, her throat hurt so much.

He crossed the room, running an impatient hand through his hair. 'Where do you want me to start? I told you I found you attractive. You're very feminine, yet surprisingly capable, highly intelligent and poised enough to cope with most situations. In fact I envy you your ease with people; it comes from growing up in a large family, I suppose. You're loyal, not afraid to stand up for yourself or to defend others, so I could add courage to the things that appeal to me.'

She supposed they were all compliments, yet they came across as coldly clinical observations, not virtues he was pleased to find in a much-loved wife. Mirry began to shiver.

But he hadn't finished. 'And then there's Wenlow. You know the house *and* the community. You belong there, and in spite of all I was brought up to believe, I find I want to belong there, too. Having you as my wife will go a long way to wiping out the stigma of being born on the wrong side of the blanket.'

Mirry listened to him, his words hitting her like stones, and she remembered Kate's warning. She was bleeding all over the floor and he wasn't even aware of it. 'And love, Jay?' she croaked. 'Where does that come in your catalogue of reasons?'

For a moment he looked baffled, then his silvery eyes gleamed. 'You mean this?' He sat down beside her, one hand sliding beneath her hair, the other drawing her against him. 'I knew that first morning at Wenlow when you got the sofa stuck on the stairs and turned on me like a fighting cock that you'd be fiery in bed,' he murmured against her ear. 'Surely you know by now you affect me more than any woman I've ever known.'

He was still using the wrong script, Mirry thought sadly. In fact, it was as if she had strayed into the wrong play, so far apart were their perceptions of love. Yet, though her mind was still reeling from the blows he had dealt, her body was helplessly responding to his touch, begging for the delights he had taught it to crave, refusing to accept that the closeness of their lovemaking was an illusion.

And, as the ripples of exquisite pleasure finally receded, even her mind clung to a last frail hope as she asked, 'Jay, if I *didn't* have five brothers, would you still have married me?'

One arm pulled her into the curve of his now lax body and he said sleepily, 'What sort of question is that? You have, so what's the point of supposing?'

The point being that she had no actual blood tie with those brothers, shared no genes, she thought miserably, trying to screw up the courage to tell him. But what should she say? You haven't cornered the market in illegitimacy, Jay? And then go on to tell him that the mother who had given her birth had been a sixteen-year-old kid taken in by the Greys as a foster child, who had then got herself killed riding pillion on her boyfriend's motorbike when Mirry was only a few weeks old? That *that* had been the way the Greys had got their 'Little Miracle', the daughter they had always wanted, when they had been allowed to legally adopt her?

As she rehearsed the phrases, Jay's deep, even breathing told her he had fallen asleep. Her confession would have to be postponed. But, though that gave her a measure of relief, Mirry was farther from sleep than she had ever been in her life, Jay's cool, emotionless reasoning crashing around inside her skull.

How could she reconcile the ardent, possessive lover with the man who had emotionlessly admitted he had married her for such cold-blooded reasons? As little more than a brood mare! Even though he had never given her the words, she had been sure he *did* love her—until tonight. And where did they go from here? When she told him in the morning how mistaken he had been in his assumptions, would he demand a divorce? The idea appalled her.

Yet now she knew his true feelings—or lack of them—why should the thought of ending the marriage give her such anguish? By rights, when he had so unfeelingly trodden her love for him beneath his feet, he should have killed it. Painfully examining her feelings, she knew that love was still alive; bruised, battered, disillusioned, but still strong enough to view the prospect of spending the rest of her life without him unbearable.

That was when she found herself wondering if it was really necessary to confess to Jay at all. If the subject had come up *before* they were married, then of course she would have told him the truth. But they were already married, their vows made before God, vows Mirry at least had made with every intention of keeping.

But wouldn't keeping silent be deceitful? her conscience argued. A lie by omission? If anyone had been deceitful, she justified herself, it was Jay, leading her to believe he had married her for love.

She cried then, tears seeping silently from beneath her closed eyelids to run down into the pillow. She cried for herself and her shattered dreams of a marriage as close and happy as her parents'. She cried for Jay, whose lonely and unloved childhood had turned him into a man who was incapable of loving.

And at last she slept, waking at first light and going to the bathroom to wash the traces of her tears away. Reaching into the bathroom cabinet, she took out the remaining pills and deliberately dropped them into the waste bin, a tacit admission of her intention to keep silent, telling herself that, just because she wasn't related by blood to the parents who had produced five boys, it didn't mean to say she wouldn't be able to produce at least one male child herself, and the sooner she began trying, the better.

She was quietly packing for the flight home when Jay woke, disgruntled to find that for the first time she wasn't still beside him. When his command that she come straight back to bed wasn't immediately obeyed, he came to fetch her and, as she had last night, Mirry melted in the heat of his lovemaking.

It hurt to know that for Jay this beautiful communion went no deeper than sexual attraction, when for herself each time was an affirmation of her love. And when she would have cried that love aloud in the cataclysm of sensation, that hurt now kept her silent. It was a love Jay had no use for, so she would keep it to herself in future. But *she* would know it was there, the hidden framework of their life together, the buried foundation of their childrens' lives.

However, having grown up in a large, uninhibitedly affectionate family and been accustomed to expressing her feelings by word and gesture, over the next few weeks Mirry found suppressing her love for Jay far more difficult than she had anticipated. She was very busy, and that helped. The builder and plumber had fulfilled their promise of completing the kitchen alterations and the new heating system by their return—the prospect of work on the flat conversions dangled before them as a carrot to produce their best efforts—but both firms were still in the house installing the bathrooms. It had been Mirry's task to supervise the clearing of both rooms before they began, and it would be for her to organise the decorators when they had finished. In the meantime she was concentrating on redesigning the master suite, turning Georgie's sitting-room into a bedroom she and Jay would share and the original bedroom into a nursery, a testament of faith in an uncertain future when it was too early yet to know if she had managed to conceive, but a gesture that pleased Jay.

Mirry enjoyed deciding which piece of antique furniture should go where, what to keep and what—reluctantly—to discard, for there was all the furniture in both wings that there would be no room for in the portion of the house remaining to them, and would either have to be stored or sent to the sale-rooms.

Jay was often away, sometimes in London, sometimes elsewhere in the country, though he managed to get home most evenings, even when it entailed a long drive after a day's work and arriving in time to go to bed. But Mirry found his comings and goings a mixed blessing, for though when he left she was able to relax the leash she had imposed on her naturally loving nature, she still missed him painfully, and when he returned she was back to the strain of keeping up a cool front.

It was like a worm at the heart of an apple, eating away at her unseen, quenching her sparkle, making her strung up and liable to flashes of irritation, as when her mother remonstrated with her, finding her trying to carry a heavy chair from one of the wings into the main house by herself.

The hurt surprise on her mother's face had her apologising at once, but Cathy still looked anxious. 'Mirry, everything *is* all right, isn't it? You're not regretting——'

'No!' Mirry's hurried denial had a note of panic in it. She was aware of the reservations her parents had had about her marriage, but it wasn't only pride that made it impossible to confide her difficulties. There was her instinctive loyalty to Jay. Besides, she was no longer a

child to go crying to her mother when the going got
rough.

'No, of *course* I'm not regretting anything, Mum,' she
said more quietly. 'It's just that Jay had to fly off to
Ireland in a hurry this morning. He won't be home tonight, either, and I——'

'And you're already missing him.' Her mother's
anxiety melted into an understanding smile. 'But, Mirry,
I'm sure Jay wouldn't want you lugging heavy stuff like
this around. If you'll wait till lunch time, I'll ask Andrew
to help.' Cathy took her arm and led her firmly to the
kitchen where Martha had the coffee ready.

'I wanted to ask Andrew if he was going to the jazz
club tonight and if I could beg a lift,' Mirry said. Ever
since the last concert for Georgie, the jazz club had been
meeting at the Greyhound in Great Wiston.

'Why don't you have dinner with us tonight if Jay
won't be home?' her mother suggested. 'William and
Eleanor are coming, so you can all go to the jazz club
together.'

The following evening Mirry was just starting down
the stairs when she heard the front door slam and Jay's
footsteps crossing the hall. She had spent the day completing the transformation of the old master suite and
moving all their things out of the bedroom they had been
using temporarily. The excitement of having a surprise
for him made her long to hurl herself down the stairs
and into his arms. Only by exercising the utmost restraint was she able to keep walking calmly downwards.

But, before she could say a word, Jay, darkly
frowning, rapped out, 'Where were you last night? I
phoned and there was no reply, so I know you were out.'

'Yes, I was. It was jazz club night,' she reminded him, wondering what he was so fussed about.

His frown deepened. 'You went to Great Wiston—on your own?'

'As it happens, no. I had dinner at the Dower House first, then the five of us, William and Eleanor, Nick and Andrew and I, all went together. Though why you should worry about me going to Great Wiston...'

Her voice trailed away, because if it *had* been her safety he was concerned about, the fact that she had been well protected failed to placate him.

'So you run home to your family the minute I'm away.' His hands grasped her shoulders, dragging her against him, his mouth descending on hers with bruising pressure. 'Perhaps that'll remind you you're my wife now.'

Mirry stared at him, her mouth throbbing from his assault. He couldn't be *jealous*, could he? Not of her brothers? And then he groaned, pulling her back into his arms, his kiss gentler this time, but deepening to a hunger she couldn't help responding to. Maybe it was knowing her brothers *did* love her that was making him possessive, she thought sadly.

It was little less than a week later that something happened to change Mirry's whole attitude to her marriage. Jay had spent the day in London and at five o'clock she had a call from his secretary to say he had just left, so when he still hadn't arrived by nine o'clock she was frantic with worry, imagining him trapped in a tangled heap of metal in a motorway pile-up. Four hours to do a trip that usually took less than two! There couldn't be any other explanation.

Unable to sit, she prowled around the house, her hand several times hovering over the phone to call up some moral support, but each time afraid to have the line busy if someone tried to reach her.

And as she prowled she prayed childishly, please God, don't let him be dead. I'll do anything, if only you'll send him back to me...

CHAPTER ELEVEN

MIRRY watched, seemingly for hours, the occasional car headlights passing along the road, and when at last one did turn into the drive, her feet hardly touched the ground as she sped along the passages and across the hall, flinging open the front door just as Jay climbed out of the car.

All thought of restraint fled as she hurtled down the steps and straight into his arms, clinging to him to reassure herself he was real and not a figment of her imagination. As he enfolded her against the solid warmth of his body, the tears started.

'Oh, Jay...I've been so *worried*!' she choked. 'Imagining the most dreadful things...an accident, and you——' Not even with Jay safely in her arms could she put into words the worst of her fears.

'There *was* an accident,' Jay said, then, feeling her convulsive shudder, 'Oh, I wasn't involved, but it closed all three carriageways for a time. I just had to sit it out till things got moving again.'

She raised her tear-stained face. These last traumatic hours had shown her just how much she loved him, how little her life would mean without him. And she saw just how mean-minded and dishonest she had been, trying to put restraints on that love, trying to stunt its growth, even deny its existence. She was ashamed of her behaviour, as if she had been saying, if you won't love me, then I won't love you. As if she had been trying to punish him, when in fact it had been herself she was hurting, twisting her own nature out of true. Love, real love, wasn't like that. It wasn't a bargaining counter, it shouldn't even demand a return. It just was.

'Tears, Mirry?' Jay sounded surprised.

'Relief, happiness that you're home and safe.' She curved her hands around his face, her lips trembling into a smile. 'You see, I love you very much, Jay, and for a few hours tonight I was afraid I'd lost you.' She immediately felt a sense of release.

A strange expression flickered in Jay's silvery eyes, one she couldn't identify. If it was embarrassment, then it was something he would have to get used to, she thought, because from now on she was going to be open and honest with her feelings.

Tucking her hand beneath his arm, she urged him into the house. 'You must be starving. Martha left us a meal ready, so you've just time for a quick shower while I heat it up in the microwave.'

'Yes, boss. Just as you say, boss.' Jay grinned at her, then kissed her hard before taking the stairs two at a time. Mirry stood for a few moments, listening to him whistling.

The sound of Jay whistling became a common occurrence over the next few weeks, for, rather than showing embarrassment at Mirry's natural expression of her feelings, it seemed to cause him some satisfaction. He still had to spend quite some time away from home, but made no objection when Mirry greeted his return by flying into his arms. Nor, when he was working at home, did he turn away from the kiss and hug that accompanied every cup of coffee she took him. If Jay didn't love her, he seemed happy enough to be loved by her.

Even their lovemaking took on a new dimension now she was no longer holding back, no longer resenting her helpless response to him. If only she could conceive a child! Because only when she had given him the first of his sons would she feel really safe, no longer haunted by the fear that someone could let slip the fact that she was the Greys' adopted daughter.

'A break will do you good,' Cathy Grey encouraged when Mirry told her she would be spending the rest of that week in London with Jay. 'Though I must say...' she examined her daughter's radiant face '...you've been looking much better lately.'

Mirry had good cause for her radiance, for it had been Jay's own suggestion that she should accompany him. It was almost as if he found the prospect of a three-day separation as intolerable as she did. And, as if that wasn't enough cause for rejoicing, her period was three days late!

Mirry chattered happily throughout the journey about what she planned to do: to get in touch with Kate, and Simon too if he was in the country, choose some new chintz at Colefax and Fowler, do a bit of personal shopping, too, something rather special for her father's birthday.

Jay smiled tolerantly, but before he left her at the Barbican flat he warned, 'Not *too* much rushing about, Mirry. Ask the porter to ring for a cab whenever you go out.'

Mirry agreed demurely, hiding her excitement. She was bursting to tell him there was a very good reason why

she shouldn't overdo things, but it *could* be a false alarm.
Better not to raise his hopes too soon.

In the flat Mirry unpacked then picked up the phone
and dialled Wren Interiors' number. Kate was delighted
to hear from her and they arranged to meet for lunch.
Half an hour later Jay called to say the head of the
American consortium he was hoping to do a deal with
wanted to meet her, and they were both invited to dine
with him that evening.

A call to Simon's flat elicited no reply, but at lunch
Kate was able to tell her he was due home the following
day, and suggested they all four got together for dinner
at her home.

Altogether it was an action-packed and very happy
few days for Mirry. Even though Jay didn't know her
secret, he was sensitive enough to her wishes and comfort
to prompt Kate to comment as Mirry helped her clear
away after the meal, 'So you were right and I was wrong,
Mirry. I hardly know Jay any more. He certainly isn't
blind to *your* feelings.'

Mirry thought about that as, tired but contented, she
and Jay drove back to Wenlow on the Friday afternoon,
his business successfully completed. It was true, Jay *had*
begun to consider her feelings. Even more, he seemed
to be doing his utmost to please her. And, if he had
made that much progress, wasn't it possible that in time
he could come to love her, too? Not just as the mother
of the sons he so urgently wanted, but for herself? Maybe
learning she was pregnant would be another step along
the way. She fell to wondering how soon she could go
to the doctor to confirm her hopes.

So it was in a particularly optimistic mood that Mirry
arrived home, to be met by an agitated Martha. 'Oh,

Mr Jay, I didn't know what to do with you not being here. She arrived last night and just…well, I could hardly throw her out, could I?'

While Mirry and Jay were trying to decipher her ramblings, a new voice drawled, 'Much as she wanted to!'

They turned simultaneously towards the voice, and as Mirry stared at the bone-thin, elegantly dressed woman standing in the library doorway she felt Jay stiffen.

'Mother!'

Mirry's eyes widened, for this woman didn't look old enough to be Jay's mother, until closer scrutiny revealed the skin stretched tautly over the facial bones as if it had undergone more than one face-lift, and the rather improbable golden blonde of her hair. So *this* was Valerie Elphick, she thought curiously.

'What on earth are you doing here?' Jay whispered.

'Now, what sort of a welcome is that for your mother?' Valerie drawled, taking it upon herself to dismiss the hovering housekeeper with a sharp, 'That will be all, Mrs Barks.'

Martha glared her affront and addressed herself to Mirry. 'Would you and Mr Jay like some tea, madam?'

Mirry had to stifle a giggle. Never in her life had Martha addressed her so formally, but to save her face she said, 'Indeed we would, Martha. Tea for three, and we'll have it in the library.' Having established who was mistress, Martha trotted back to the kitchen.

'Perhaps we could all sit down, Mrs…' Mirry hesitated. 'I'm sorry, I don't know your married name.'

Valerie inclined her head graciously. 'Ginsher. Mrs *Oscar* Ginsher,' she stressed, as if that should mean something to them. When no reaction was forthcoming she fished a wisp of handkerchief from her sleeve and carefully dabbed the corners of her eyes. 'Such a dear man, but not...' She paused significantly. 'I lost him six months ago, and without him...well, it was no great sacrifice to sell up in California and come home to Wenlow.'

'Home, Mother?' Jay asked cynically, fast recovering from his shock. 'As far as I know you never spent longer than three months here, so I fail to see how you can look on it as home.'

Mirry, listening with a sinking feeling in her stomach, watched Valerie shake her head sorrowfully. 'I can't really expect you to understand just what your father— and this place—meant to me.'

'So much that you brought me up to hate him?' Jay's cynicism deepened.

Valerie gave a muffled sob. 'Oh, that was wrong of me, I know that now. But when everything was against us—his wife, her family—I was so hurt that he didn't stand out against them so I lashed back at him.' She raised her head, and as she looked pleadingly at her son Mirry saw there were real tears in her eyes. 'Believe me, if I had my time over again...'

'Please don't upset yourself, Mrs Ginsher.' Mirry urged her into a chair. If Valerie now regretted her behaviour in the past, Mirry for one wasn't going to hold it against her.

Valerie allow herself to be seated, smiling up at Mirry tremulously. 'Thank you, my dear. I'm afraid I have no idea who you are.'

'This very tender-hearted lady,' Jay said, crossing the room and curving a protective arm round Mirry's waist, 'is my wife, Mirry.'

'Your *wife*?' Valerie looked shaken. 'I'd no idea you were married!'

'Just as I had no idea you'd been widowed,' Jay pointed out sardonically. 'We've been married a little over two months.'

'Newly-weds!' Valerie said faintly. 'How lovely!' Yet Mirry got the distinct impression the news wasn't welcome.

Martha interrupted with the tea trolley then, and by the time she departed Valerie seemed to have recovered from her shock. 'Mirry... That's an unusual name.'

'A pet name,' Jay said before Mirry could respond, 'and one that suits her to a tee. Her given names are Georgina Catherine.' Mirry saw he was watching his mother with sardonic amusement. 'Georgina after her godmother, Lady Jayston, and Catherine after her mother, Cathy Grey.'

Mirry could see the shock on Valerie's face, and couldn't share Jay's amusement. The taut skin whitened, leaving the blusher standing out like a clown's make-up. 'I see.' At last Valerie broke the tense silence. She put down her cup and rose gracefully to her feet. 'Then I can understand that she won't be able to find a welcome for me in her home.'

Moved to pity, and impressed by Valerie's quiet dignity, Mirry assured her with impulsive warmth, 'Oh, but of course you're welcome, isn't she, Jay? We can't change the past, but we can give it a decent burial.'

'I don't know if encouraging her to stay was a good idea,' Jay said later when they were alone. 'I got the impression she'd come here ready to step in as Lady of the Manor, and wasn't at all pleased to find the role filled.'

'But I thought she took it very well when she discovered I was a Grey,' Mirry demurred. 'In fact, she seemed more concerned that I wouldn't be able to accept *her* than the other way around.'

'Now, that *did* surprise me. If I could be sure she really has changed...' He looked so uncertain that Mirry's heart went out to him. Whatever painful childhood memories Valerie's unexpected arrival had raised, she was still his mother.

'Darling...' She wound her arms around his waist. 'You were a child in a situation you couldn't begin to understand. Now you'll have the chance to get to know her as an adult.'

Jay still looked uncertain. 'And what about your parents? I told them there was no chance of her ever coming here.'

Remembering their prejudice, Mirry felt a qualm, but subdued it firmly. 'They'll understand, Jay. The situation's different now. David and Georgie are both gone, so there's no one who can be hurt.'

She wasn't to know how wrong she was.

At first Valerie seemed pathetically grateful to be allowed this visit to Wenlow, deferring prettily to Mirry, and if she expressed horror when she learned of the plans to convert two-thirds of the house into flats, she followed up quickly with, 'Of course it all belongs to you now, Jay, and you must do as you think best.'

But as the days passed Mirry found her mother-in-law's continuing presence severely curtailed the work she still had to do refurbishing the house, especially when Valerie's praise for what she had achieved was qualified by her plaintive, 'Of course, it's not to my taste.'

So, after having Valerie dogging her heels, slipping in her little digs, Mirry was relieved when she hired a car to make trips to Leicester and Market Harborough, and sometimes took walks around the village, even spending the odd evening in the village pub.

'Renewing old acquaintances,' she claimed, and at the same time giving the newly-weds some time on their own.

'But how long does she intend to stay?' Cathy Grey asked when Mirry escaped for an hour one day to the Dower House. Although Martha had warned Donald and Cathy of Valerie's arrival even before Mirry and Jay knew of it, they had as yet had no contact with her.

Mirry sighed, wondering that herself. She wanted to make an appointment with the doctor to get her pregnancy confirmed, but she was strangely reluctant to break the news to Jay while his mother was still in the house. But she said lightly, 'Oh, she's only been here just over a week, and it *is* twelve years since she last saw Jay.'

She sighed again, admitting to herself her relationship with Jay had taken a step backwards since his mother's arrival. He was still solicitous for her welfare, but there were times when he withdrew from her behind his old wooden expression. And, though she often saw him watching his mother, she still didn't know how he felt about her, if they had grown any closer, because whenever she prompted him he returned only bland, uninformative replies. Certainly Valerie spent time with him when Mirry wasn't there, but he never told her what had passed between them.

'Odd how she only wanted to see him again after she heard he'd inherited Wenlow. And how *did* she hear, I wonder?' Cathy said darkly, then, with an anxious glance

at her daughter, asked, 'She's not making trouble between you and Jay, is she?'

Mirry shook her head. On the surface at least, Valerie
seemed to have accepted her son's marriage into the Grey
family without rancour, though sometimes Mirry had
the uneasy feeling she was playing a part. Or rather, many
parts: the remorseful mother regretting past mistakes;
the mother-in-law trying hard to be tolerant; the exile
returned to a well-loved home. But just now and again
Mirry had caught a glimpse of something else. Little
things, like a too-peremptory order to Martha, or a
hastily bitten back criticism of herself. Yet, though Jay
seemed . . . different when she was around, Mirry had to
admit Valerie had done nothing overt to cause trouble.

'I suppose we must bow to the inevitable,' Cathy said
resignedly. 'She is your mother-in-law, and if it's going
to make things more comfortable for you and Jay, your
father and I are ready to forget past grievances. You'd
better bring her along for dinner tonight.'

It was with a similar attitude of conciliation that
Valerie accepted the invitation, much to Mirry's relief,
and she prepared for the evening with a light heart. She
knew Valerie had come equipped with an extensive and
very elegant wardrobe, so not to be outdone Mirry chose
a dress she would normally have considered a bit over
the top for a family dinner, a pretty floral chiffon in
greens and golds with narrow bootlace shoulder-straps.

In a superbly cut black silk dress and impossibly high-
heeled shoes, there was no way they could expect Valerie
to walk the path between the two properties, so Jay
fetched the car out, transporting them from door to door
in style.

It quickly became apparent that Valerie was playing the part of the sorrowing widow for this renewal of acquaintance with Donald and Cathy Grey, making no reference at all to the time she had worked as a secretary at Wenlow thirty years before. And Donald and Cathy were only too happy not to raise the subject. They listened as Valerie told them what a wonderful husband her Oscar had been, and asked polite questions about her life in America. That took them safely through predinner drinks, and when they were all settled round the table sampling Cathy's soup made from asparagus grown in her own garden, Donald asked Valerie about her plans.

She seemed unwilling to commit herself. 'I don't think I could bear to go back to California now my dear Oscar's gone. On the other hand, I shall miss my friends. Yet what are friends compared to one's own flesh and blood? I missed Jay so much all these years that I'm inclined to stay close now.'

'London, perhaps?' Cathy suggested, darting an anxious glance at a very wooden-faced Jay before gathering up the empty soup bowls and setting out the warmed plates.

'Ah, London! I've always loved London,' Valerie agreed. 'Oscar left me very well provided for, so that widens my choice. And there's no hurry to make up my mind.'

Mirry couldn't hide her dismay as she glanced at Jay, whose expression gave nothing away. It was her father who suggested diplomatically that maybe Valerie could spend some time in Jay's London flat while she looked around for somewhere suitable, adding with bland innocence, 'As your own marriage was so happy, I'm sure you won't blame me for reminding you every newly-wed couple need time on their own to settle down.'

'But of course. Please don't think I'm about to outstay my welcome.' Valerie fluttered her eyelashes at him, adding sweetly, 'But as you and Cathy have your daughter on your doorstep, I'm sure you won't blame *me* for wanting to stay close to my son.' She gave a tinkling laugh. 'Why, I might even decide to buy one of those flats he's planning at the Hall.'

'They're still very much in the planning stage, Mother,' Jay pointed out. 'We haven't applied for planning permission yet.'

Something flickered in Valerie's light eyes. Mirry would have expected anger at Jay's apparently trying to put her off, yet it looked oddly like satisfaction. 'Then maybe I shall buy a permanent home in London and one of the flats here later as a *pied-à-terre*,' she said carelessly. 'That way I can see my son without upsetting his wife.'

'I don't think anyone has suggested your visit has upset Mirry, Mother,' Jay said coolly.

'But of course not, dear.' Valerie looked helplessly flustered. 'I must have put it badly. I meant, so that I won't be intruding on either of you.' Then she said to Cathy as she was offered the sauce-boat, 'Do your children pick you up on every word? I seem to remember you had two small boys.'

'I finished up with five,' Cathy laughed.

'Five?' Valerie opened her eyes wide. 'Five boys to cope with, yet you still went ahead and adopted Mirry!'

Mirry froze in her chair. It was something that had haunted her ever since the last night of her honeymoon, the possibility that the subject of her adoption might come up, yet that it should do so tonight was utterly unexpected.

Her eyes flew to Jay's face, seeing his shock as Valerie pursued with gentle persistence, 'She was, wasn't she? Adopted, I mean?'

'Yes, it's never been any secret. Mirry was the little girl we'd always longed for and had given up hoping to achieve.' Cathy smiled fondly at her daughter, but Mirry's gaze hadn't moved from Jay's face. And when he met her eyes it was with such an appalled expression that she slid quietly from her chair in a dead faint.

She didn't see Jay leap to his feet so violently that his chair crashed backwards to reach her before her father did, nor hear her mother's startled shriek. And none of them noticed the rather surprised satisfaction on Valerie's face, for Jay's mother had drawn a bow at a venture and had somehow managed to hit a bull's-eye.

Mirry came to groggily to find herself in her own bed at Wenlow, with Doctor Alton bending over her and her mother hovering at his shoulder. 'How did I——' she faltered, wondering if that scene at her mother's dinner-table had been a bad dream.

'I wanted to put you to bed at the Dower House, but Jay insisted on bringing you home,' her mother said. 'Now just lie still, Mirry, while the doctor takes a look at you.'

Jay may have insisted on bringing her home, but he wasn't with her now, Mirry noticed, and that fact seemed to say it all. She lay still while the doctor pulled down her eyelids, then shone a light into her eyes.

'Any idea what made you pass out?' he asked.

She knew her mother would have to know the truth eventually, but she couldn't face the doctor knowing too, so she used the only other excuse available to her. 'I—I think I might be pregnant.'

She saw the relief and delight in her mother's face even as the doctor gave an understanding, 'Ah!'

'I was going to come and see you,' she hastened to add, 'but I thought it might be too soon.' She glanced at her mother. 'I haven't even told Jay yet.' And when she did, would he grant a stay of execution while he waited to see if she produced a son? She couldn't get that appalled expression she had seen on his face out of her mind.

'I'm going to leave some iron tablets with you now,' the doctor said, 'and in the morning I expect you to ring the surgery and make an appointment.' He counted out some pills into a box and snapped his bag shut. 'And the best treatment I can recommend is plenty of TLC from your husband,' he finished jovially as he moved to the door.

Tender loving care. The last thing she was likely to get from Jay now. Mirry squeezed her eyes shut to stem the tears. 'I'm sorry I made a shambles of your dinner party, Mum,' she said as a movement by the bed reminded her she wasn't alone.

'As if that matters,' Cathy dismissed. 'I think you should sleep now, darling. Would you like me to stay?'

It was tempting to revert to childhood again, to lay her burden of pain on her mother's shoulders and have her make everything better. But this was something only she and Jay could work out between them. 'Thanks, Mum, but I'll be fine. You get home and tell Dad there's nothing to worry about.'

'As if that'll stop him,' her mother laughed. 'And you'd better tell Jay your news, even if you haven't had

it confirmed yet. He looked like a man whose last
moment had come when you collapsed like that.'

But Mirry knew it wasn't her collapse that had caused
his consternation.

'She says she's feeling better, Jay,' her mother said,
and then he was there in the doorway, his face white and
rigid, only his eyes alive, glittering with a fierce emotion
Mirry knew could only be anger.

He closed the door behind him. 'You still look very
pale.' Watching him apprehensively as he walked stiffly
towards the bed, Mirry didn't comment. 'My mother's
packing,' he said with harsh abruptness.

'Your *mother's* packing?' The unexpectedness of it
prompted a near hysterical laugh. 'And here I was
expecting you to tell *me* to go!'

'Mirry...' His voice sounded strangled and her hys-
teria died to leave her feeling numb and empty, drained
of all emotion.

'I'm sorry, Jay,' she said remotely. 'I should have told
you about my adoption as soon as I knew how important it had suddenly become, but we were already
married by then and I hoped——'

'*You're* sorry?' Jay slid to his knees beside the bed
and gripped her hand. 'My God! It's not you who has
anything to be sorry about, it's I who should be begging
you to forgive me. As I am now...on my knees.'

'Jay...?' Mirry stared at him wonderingly, unconscious of the pain of his grip. 'But I thought...you told
me why you married me...and when your mother...
Jay, you looked so *appalled*!'

'Of course I was appalled,' he said roughly. 'I was
remembering all those things I'd said, realising how much
I must have hurt you, knowing exactly why you were

looking so stricken. When you collapsed...' He squeezed his eyes shut.

He didn't sound now like the man Kate had described as having a blind spot to other people's feelings. Perhaps there was some hope for them, after all. 'You—you don't want to end our marriage, then?'

'God, no!' His answer came explosively. 'Anything but that.' Only then did he realise he was crushing her much smaller hand and release his grip, gentling the marked skin with both of his and missing the flood of relief in Mirry's face. 'The things I told you about why I married you...' He kept his gaze on their joined hands. 'They were all true, but they weren't the whole truth. There was so much more that I couldn't—didn't know how to say. Even now...'

'Oh, Jay...' Mirry's eyes were glowing with compassion and tenderness, and her free hand reached out to caress his downbent head, curving round to his cheek. 'I think I understand what you're trying to say. I've been so lucky, growing up part of a loving family. It's been easy for me to love you. But your childhood was so different. I can understand if you find it hard.'

He took her into his arms, holding her convulsively, his face pressed against her hair. 'I only know you're like the sun, like a flame,' he said thickly. 'The source of all warmth. When I'm away I can't wait to get back to you. I feel...*different* when I'm with you. I want to laugh more, make *you* laugh. Make you happy. and I can't bear to think of a world without you at its centre.'

'Oh, darling...' Mirry laughed gently, though she felt nearer to tears. 'You've just described exactly what it's like to be in love.'

He moved back a little so he could look down into her face, for the first time his expression open to his emotion. 'In that case, I love you, Mirry.' He pulled her close again, whispering against her ear like a vow, 'I love you...I love you...' as if having started to say it he couldn't stop. Even when Mirry pulled his head down to kiss him, he still said the words into her mouth, continued to say them while his hands and mouth worshipped her, cried them aloud as their bodies joined, and again as the world splintered into shining fragments around them.

'My God! What have I done?' he panted raggedly when the breath returned to his lungs.

'It seemed very much as if you were *showing* me how much you love me,' Mirry teased lovingly, knowing she would always think of this night as the true beginning of their marriage, when both their hearts had been open to each other without fear or restraint.

'But not an hour ago you were unconscious!' Jay exclaimed worriedly. 'I shouldn't have——'

'Of course you should,' Mirry contradicted. 'As if loving me could ever hurt me. Besides, I only fainted because I could be pregnant, and I'm not going to let that stop——'

'Pregnant?' Jay shot up in bed and stared at her as if he'd just been sand-bagged. Then, with a dawning look of wonder, 'You're having my child?'

'The first of our sons,' Mirry said determinedly.

Jay flopped back against the pillow, tightening his arms around her. 'Sons, hell! I want a little girl...just like you.'

If Mirry had had any lingering doubts about Jay's feelings, those words would have dispelled them. They were what she had yearned to hear that traumatic last night of their honeymoon, and they told her that what she had always wanted was hers at last, a marriage like her parents had, built on a love so deep that it spilled over on to all who touched it, children, family and friends. She could even feel it in her heart to tolerate her mother-in-law...in small doses.

'You'll have what you get,' she told him, laughing, 'and love it anyway.'

'Yes.' Jay gave a sigh of pure contentment. 'But you'll always be the most precious thing in my life, Mirry. Mirry... No wonder that name stuck. You *are* a miracle. My very own miracle...'

Harlequin Presents

Coming Next Month

#1255 EVER SINCE EDEN Catherine George
Clemency falls in love with Nicholas Wood at a fancy-dress ball—a fact confirmed the next day There seems no reason their fairy-tale romance shouldn't continue indefinitely So Clemency is devastated when, suddenly and brutally, Nick changes his mind.

#1256 LAW OF LOVE Sally Heywood
Kim is bowled over by barrister Con Arlington's looks and charm—until she discovers he is really Conan Arlington-Forbes, the man she's held a grudge against for five years   with good reason!

#1257 ONCE A HERO Anne McAllister
Lesley had built a satisfying new life for herself before her husband, Matt Colter, reappeared, causing her more pain than joy Matt had always put his work before their marriage, and she has no reason to believe he's changed.

#1258 ELUSIVE AS THE UNICORN Carole Mortimer
Eve refuses to believe Adam when he says she'd be making a mistake marrying Paul Even though their names seem to indicate an affinity between them, Adam is a total stranger and has no right to interfere in her life.

#1259 BLACK LION OF SKIAPELOS Annabel Murray
When Helena meets Marcos Mavroleon she isn't looking for a relationship, simply trying to mend a broken heart. His complex personality draws her close—yet his traditional streak means that he can never be hers.

#1260 TASMANIAN DEVIL Valerie Parv
Evelyn agrees to fend for herself for a month on a tiny island—to prove herself capable to her father Expecting to be alone, she finds the enigmatic Dane Balkan already there He seems as unhappy with her presence as she is with his.

#1261 SKIN DEEP Kay Thorpe
Tessa enjoys working with children but makes it a rule never to get emotionally involved with her charges. In her present case, though, it isn't young Jason causing her upsets, but his attractive, aggressive father, Mark Leyland

#1262 GUARDIAN ANGEL Patricia Wilson
Tara dislikes her overpowering boss, Ben Shapiro, even though she's grateful for his kindness to her disabled mother It does seem strange, though, that every time she meets Ben, sparks fly between them

Available in April wherever paperback books are sold, or through Harlequin Reader Service·

In the U.S.
901 Fuhrmann Blvd.
P O. Box 1397
Buffalo, N.Y 14240-1397

In Canada
P.O. Box 603
Fort Erie, Ontario
L2A 5X3

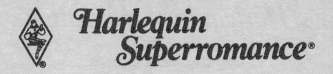

Harlequin Superromance®

LET THE GOOD TIMES ROLL . . .

Add some Cajun spice to liven up your New Year's celebrations and join Superromance for a romantic tour of the rich Acadian marshlands and the legendary Louisiana bayous.

CAJUN MELODIES, starting in January 1990, is a three-book tribute to the fun-loving people who've enriched America by introducing us to crawfish étouffé and gumbo, zydeco music and the Saturday night party, the *fais-dodo*. And learn about loving, Cajun-style, as you meet the tall, dark, handsome men who win their ladies' hearts with a beautiful, haunting melody. . . .

Book One: *Julianne's Song*, January 1990
Book Two: *Catherine's Song*, February 1990
Book Three: *Jessica's Song*, March 1990